WORLD OF OKRIA
THE SEVEN TRIALS

KRITIKOS SARANTIS

WORLD OF OKRIA

THE SEVEN TRIALS

Translation from Greek

DORA CHATZAKOU

YMOS PUBLICATIONS

SYMI 2014

Cover design: Sarantis Kritikos

Available from Amazon.com and other book stores
Available on Kindle and other devices

worldofokria.com
kritikossarantis.com

Thanks

Jon Araque - proof reading

Stamatis Kritikos

Dedicated to my grandson

22/10/14

Chapter 1

With a feeling of disgust I looked at what I had started writing on the piece of paper and then I took it and made a ball out of it inside my palms. I was really upset with the whole situation. I bent my head again to think but the thoughts were running. I was incapable of catching one of them and transfer it on the piece of paper. I raised my fist and hit the table so hard that I made (really hard making) all the objects on it jump.

Damn society! Everyone is good-mannered; having a conventional smile just for the occasion. They have a forced courtesy which hides what's in the inside' like sour cream and fancy wrapping paper do but when you try it, it makes you spit. Together with the stones you didn't think existed, making for some broken teeth too.

I reconsidered it again, but in vain. I had to play their game. I had to repeat the words I didn't feel like saying and, if possible, bite them while uttering them out of my mouth. Damn society, I say that again! Unfair God. Mean. Devastating you, stepping on you, making you crawl and beg without paying attention to you.

The best are given to the evil and mean leaving the rubbish to us. When you try to talk to anyone, all you get is excuses and botches for a life that passes in front of your eyes like bolt. And hope runs even faster than logic making you wait and long for.

You know the result. Still, you never decide to unroot the hope that misguides you every time and adds even more feelings to the scale. Every time you say 'This is the last time! I won't listen to the Sirines again', you end up getting lost in fake promises. When will I grow up? When?

Chapter 2

The wind from the road blew on my face making me think of the situation in a cooler temper. I had no other choice, though. I had to do what I hated; to beg and crawl for a damn job.

What job was it anyway? Maybe work for someone who made plastic like they told me. And now I had to beg some politician of influence. To give whatever it took for him so that he would plead for me with the employer. This was a chain which I had to drag myself to make the system move; becoming one of its rings against my will.

I looked at my face on a shop window. Nothing important. The same again and again. I put my fingers in my hair from both sides and looked again on the shop window. Should I have it cut? No. It had a deeper meaning. It was a matter of freedom. With my hair long I felt like a wild horse ready to pour out in the fields but that moment was yet to come.

Unfortunately, whatever I did I had to return to the letter I had to write. It was all because of my aunt and her obsolete ideas. I had to do it for her because I owed it to her. The letter would start like this:

"I would like to ask you to mediate so that I would get the position in the plastic's factory, whatever it was called. I am Anna's nephew who knows your friend Giorgos"…

I don't give a damn about anyone. I just can't. I have no time to waste on such things. I had better use what I have for something else. I looked at some small kids who were passing by and remembered my childhood years on the island. Poverty, misery and privation. Still those years were so sweet. I was carefree. Free without commitments, do's and don'ts, with nothing to worry about. And then everything came suddenly and unexpectedly.

My father got ill and passed away very soon thereafter. I think I was on fourth grade and the bitterness that it left me went on because what happened next made me turn in on myself. After my father had passed away, my aunt who lived in Athens advised us that we should go up there since there were many more jobs. And moreover, a single mother with a child wouldn't be able to make it on the island without any relatives. We had no other choice.

I continued going to school and my mother got a job at a textile-factory thanks to my aunt's acquaintances. Though we had been in Athens for nine years, we didn't achieve many things by trying to make a living, neither did I manage to adjust to the big city which was trying to convince me to do so in thousands of ways.

On my father's death I was crying because I was watching my mother crying. I hadn't realized exactly what death was. As the years were passing I was beginning to feel it more. But the bitterness became huge as a mountain when I had to say goodbye to my mother. That was when I realized it for good.

I remember myself crying for many days because I was left alone in a city I couldn't understand and neither could it understand me. My aunt was in bed most of the time, especially lately, I was taking her of her more than she was taking care of me and we had a one-way and one-sided communication.

I brought my life on the island back to my mind, however short it was. The perpetual sea had structured me to such an extent. Its vastness and restless motion had really formed my character even though I had only lived there for a few years. It had left its indelible stamp on me. That rock, which seemed as if it had fallen down from the sky and where I used to go to the small Marathounda beach during my stay there as a guest at a relative's house, was my most beloved memory.

I was looking at the sea thinking of far away places, like those I watched on TV. Many people, fancy colors, everything seemed so easy to acquire without trying much. I had dreams. Unfortunately, I realized that things were different in Athens.

Everything was fake - like television. It created expectations and hope to you leaving you afterwards either in a desert with hot sun or in freezing, below zero cold with no clothes. You have two choices then. Either to leave everything and go or end up having illusions created by certain substances they have sold you. To be honest I was really close to that once but an old man who lived in a ruin got me out of the trouble I was about to fall into.

"What are you trying to do boy?", he yelled at me to my face.

I replied, "I'm sick and tired of the lies."

"And do you want to fall into a bigger lie?", he asked me furiously.

I was scared. His look was throwing out sparks and his fingers were hurting me in my shoulder as he was dragging me outside.

"Go!", he said. "Go and don't think about it again!"

I turned to look at him and saw tears coming out from his eyes. I stopped and looked at him wondering. "Why?", I muttered. I couldn't understand. He swept away his tears and said, "That's how I lost my only child. They sold him fake dreams."

I was so confused. I had nothing to say. I couldn't utter a single word. I quit. I stormed out and started running as if they were running after me. As if police cars were chasing me with their sirens screaming and everyone was looking at me. I stopped hanging out with those guys before making a big mistake. Thanks to that old man. It's been a year now.

Chapter 3

Everything I had been through had carved big scars deep inside me. Nobody knew the bitterness I felt. I didn't express my feelings. But what kept me still alive was my island and my fantasy.

When I wanted to get away from reality I dived into dark corners of my mind looking for pieces of a puzzle which scared even me that I was thinking about them. And I was trying to create, with my fantasy guiding me, stories which were taking place in weird places of my island with no sun; full of mystery with heroes who achieved what was unachievable.

Having a spirit of altruism, justice, friendship and love, virtues which today's society lacks in, these heroes achieved remarkable goals always for the benefit of the whole society; that which is enclosed in secret paths and untrodden places that could exist eternally and recycle whatever material was necessary for its survival.

Many times I punished those who commit crimes in today's world and remain without punishment by giving their characters, positions and names to the evil ones of my fictional land. The ones who were bad, manipulative and who would be punished by justice and the heroes would beat them in battle. In that way I took revenge. I mocked them for all the horrible things they had done to the people and I satisfied my desire for justice even in my imagination.

This is the joy that fantasy gives you. To be able to achieve the unachievable. To hold the bad ones accountable.To bring them to justice and punish them according to the rules of morality. I remember that when I was little and the story I was reading ended, I made a new one with my own heroes. Most of the time I was one of the main characters; daring bold achievements riding my horse.

Chapter 4

I felt that the city was ready to throw me up; to wash me ashore like a useless unwanted carcass but I wouldn't give it this pleasure. Something stronger than a thousand magnets or even the gravity of the Earth was attracting me to it and I couldn't resist.

I knew what it was. It was my destiny - the desire for what I had loved the most. It was the sunlight that jumps and dances on the hot rocks. The inviting movement of the waves. The thin trees that seek moisture in vain and instead get the saltiness of the sea. It was also the lonely birds that sympathize with human beings. The legends and myths which you can feel in the air. The special name of each rock after existing among human beings. The attempt not to lose the roots throughout the centuries. The secret passages and the caves with their secrets only for the initiated. The ancestors' traits and the world of fantasy which in some parts of the island could find the ideal place to be expressed, create and fly. I made my decision. I am going to write the letter.

Chapter 5

When Michael's aunt got out of bed with difficulty she saw a big piece of paper on the bedside table with the following note written with a thick marker:

'My dearest aunt,

Thank you for everything you have done for me but I can't continue living here any more. I'm going to the island by boat. I'll call you when I get there.''

"Devil boy! He has always done whatever he wanted", she muttered and started preparing her breakfast. "Where will he go all alone?" she thought to herself. "Can he keep a house on his own?" And then continued with what she was doing.

Chapter 6

I imagined my island Symi; sailing on the sea in full sail as I remember it every time. The etesian wind blew trying to prove that it is the only one that rules the sea and if anyone dared to prove otherwise, who knows what would happen to them. Exactly like that time when I was traveling.

The boat stopped at Cyclades due to strong winds. However, this didn't bother me at all. Either that day or the following I would be in the place I was born; ready to make a new beginning in my life. The misfortunes that came one after the other and the jobs I used to do in the mornings didn't leave me with any time or interest in the night school I attended in Athens. However, I managed to finish high school and now I had to think very seriously what job suited me and would interest me to do.

I worked as a builder, a salesman in shops, and a traveling salesman, in order to help my mother and bear a part of the financial burdens; but none of it actually expressed me nor fulfilled me. Of course, when there is a need for a job you don't have the luxury to choose an occupation - it chooses you. I had other ambitions though, but I didn't know if they would be fulfilled.

I always had three books next to my pillow from which I couldn't ever separate. Those were the Iliad, the Odyssey, and Greek Mythology. I had read them countless times but each time I felt as if it were the first time. What job could I combine with this love of mine? An archaeologist maybe? But I should have planned it earlier because it required a lot of studying for the exams. But still, I wouldn't have been able to afford to finish my studies if I had entered the university, of course. Or could I become a museum attendant? Hmmm… this would suit me more. Anyway, I had to make a decision soon.

Chapter 7

I set myself to fixing my family house on the island, which was all the fortune I was left with. And my years of absence had turned it into a shelter for spiders, cockroaches and the humidity had moulded the walls and the floor. I met a few old schoolmates of mine and I remembered all my childhood until I was at fourth grade.

Time has a different pace in Symi than it does in Athens. You don't have the pressure, the stress and the agony to make it. In Symi you can postpone what you have to do. You can have a break whenever you want and in the meantime be a part of nature yourself. I couldn't wait. The following day I would start my excursions to remember and also get to know new places.

Chapter 8

I climbed up one of my favorite places of my fantasy, Okria, a mythical mountain with branches in interesting locations and from there I would go to the bay of Marathounda with its rock on the beach. Okria, together with Varouha and Dysalonas, is where all the action of my heroes took place and these were the places that stirred my imagination.

Varouha was a plateau with an ancient settlement the fortification of which is quite remarkable. It has huge carved boulders placed with great mastery and skill making it impossible, even today, to pass a knife through them. The central part of the ancient settlement is occupied by Mikros Sotiris Monastery, which is built from the old building material of the ancient buildings that used to be there. A stream separates Varouha next to which is the mountain of Okria. It is a place with caves and dwellings of prehistoric people. A place of legends and tradition, with stones from wine-presses and mills and on its foot lay two ancient ports - Nanou and Marathounda.

Dysalonas, as it is called today, used to be called Dysalotos which means 'difficult to conquest'. It is an exquisite beach which you can reach only by the sea due to its impenetrable mountains both on its left and right side and also its impressive central region where the mountain gives the impression that a knife has split it in two leaving it with a 400-meter cut. On its foot you can see the chapel of Saint Georgios the Dysalotos. After there is the vast beach with its white pebbles meeting the sea, obeying its command to do so.

I didn't know all these things, except for Dysalonas and Marathounda which I had visited with my father when I was little. He had narrated me many stories on legends and things that were said and all these had been recorded in my childhood memory .But now I wanted to see all these places closely and discover on my own not only what I had heard about them, but also what I had imagined with stories I made up.

Chapter 9

I was walking down to Marathounda where many summer houses had been built lately and it had changed a lot since the last time I had been there as a little boy. Like all the island's beaches it was full of tourists arriving there by any means they could. Either by land, through the road, or by sea in the taxi boats.

What impressed me was a little house high up on the left which I didn't remember and it didn't seem to be a summer house. When I went near it some dogs welcomed me showing me their sharp teeth making the owner of the house go out to see who was out there.

"Come in", said a suntanned man who seemed to be a shepherd.

"I'm going to the beach, you know", I replied hesitantly.

"Come in to have a glass of water and then go", he told me again as if he had known me for years.

I put my rucksack down while the dogs were lying under the shade feeling calm now that their owner had realized the presence of the unexpected visitor. I went into the courtyard and looked at a man who was there under the vine arbor.

His look impressed me. It seemed as if he wasn't looking at today; as if he didn't care at all about what was happening around him. If I were to give a title to one of his photos, I would name it "eternity". He had a calm look on his face and his eyes were gazing at nowhere. I was looking at him in curiosity because of how he looked and behaved when he went on with his conversation with the shepherd which he had stopped due to my presence.

As soon as he started talking my surprise was even bigger. I couldn't believe my ears! It was impossible! I thought that the sun had made me feel dizzy or I needed to see a psychiatrist. What I was hearing was inconceivable and beyond reality. That strange guy was narrating my own stories, the ones I had made up myself in my fantasy! It was as if he had got into my head and copied the data of my memory.

He stopped for a minute to feel the wind that was blowing from Okria as if it was bringing messages and old stories to him. As the wind was blowing through the leaves and branches it gave you the impression that it was whispering to his ear what he was narrating.

As if he had read my mind, he said, "If you listen carefully, you can hear words and sounds but only the initiated will be able to understand them."

I wanted to ask him so many things but everything was so mixed-up in my mind that I thought my words wouldn't make sense if I tried to speak. I didn't know where to begin. He went on with his narration pausing many times in order to remember a story or hear the message the wind was whispering to him.

All the stories were taking place in the north a bit higher than the place we were. I don't know if it was just my impression but while he was talking the leaves and branches of the trees seemed to be nodding and agreeing with what he was narrating. Up there in north the heroes never die. They keep on fighting through the days, years and centuries; achieving heroic feats for their people, for those who still have a special place in their heart.

There is always a hero behind every simple thing that happens, who makes it possible. That's why the heroes and their feats are so many. So that strange man's narrations are endless; a whole lifetime is not enough to narrate all of them and since he can't remember them all, he waits on the wind to bring all the secrets to him through the leaves and branches of the trees.

I felt as if hammers were hitting all over my head and I had mixed-up the past with the present. I was thinking to myself that I wouldn't escape a visit to psychiatrist. At a desperate attempt to change what was going on, even though I loved to hear about the fight between the good and the bad, I had to pretend that I had something to do and I left towards the beach after thanking the shepherd for the water. I had another plan, though. I wanted to wait for this strange guy to get out and meet him so as to solve the mystery.

I arrived at the beach but I didn't leave the little house from my eyes. After a few minutes I saw him walking with his cane towards some ruins and stopping for a while. That moment a child shouted because of something he had seen in the sea and distracted me. When I tried to see the strange guy he wasn't there. He had disappeared.

I got so mad at myself. I waited for him to appear again, but in vain. The sun was so hot that I sat under a small tree in search of shade. After feeling a bit cooler I stood up heading for the ruins where I had seen the strange visitor for the last time. When I went near I realized that they weren't simple ruins. They were ancient ruins of an ancient building or maybe a temple.

I was looking ecstatically at the huge carved rocks and the shards that were all over. I moved and then I saw something shining on my left. I looked closely and saw a round, golden, shimmering object that could fit in my palm. In its centre there was a star with six rays which were reaching its periphery and going out of it forming a triangular shape looking like a cogwheel. The other parts between the rays were empty as if there used to be other pieces there that filled the gaps of the cycle but were broken now.

I thought to take it and look more closely so I stretched out my arm, but fortunately I didn't touch it. A huge snake was around and you couldn't discern it easily because it was of the same color as the ground. I pulled my hand away feeling frightened and stepped behind looking at the golden object ecstatically. I wanted it so badly.

Suddenly the snake went away and hid behind a rock allowing me to hold the object. I took it in my hands that were shaking. I suddenly felt my eyes closing while I was immersing into a fog in which I couldn't discern anything. It was as if I was diving into a sea made of thick white fog losing my senses. I tried to resist and react but in vain. I didn't have the courage. I surrendered without knowing where I was going, clenching the strange golden object in my fist.

Chapter 10

"He is mine", someone screamed angrily.

"It's not you who will make this decision", replied another.

"No matter what you say he is mine."

"Hyperinor will decide."

"You know that Nohra has the same and even stronger power."

"You say that."

"It's all your fault because you place obstacles all the time. Otherwise Nohra would be in Hyperinor's place now."

"You always want to let evil rule."

"No, we always want the opposite opinion to rule."

"You will never convince me and neither will I."

I thought that the voices I was hearing were coming through a corridor and I still couldn't open my eyes. I was beginning to wake up from a lethargic sleep like the one you fall into after anesthesia or high fever. It's a dream, I thought to myself. I was really walking along a corridor escorted by a strangely dressed guy. It sure is a weird dream, I thought to myself again. I looked at my hand and realized that I was still holding the golden symbol really tight. What if all this is true?

In the meantime we reached the end of the corridor and climbed up a large number of stairs; at the end of which there was a door made of heavy wood which was obviously leading to a room. We entered and what we saw was a big room in which there were seven men with beards and long hair standing on a very high pedestal opposite the door.

Each of them was wearing a robe in different color from the others and the one standing in the middle was a bit taller than the rest. Below them at a lower level there were nine people, and more below twelve others and then there was a square which was crowded. Obviously, they were following a kind of hierarchy and you could tell that because of the arrangement of the seats and levels. The light was dim giving the impression it would be dawn very soon.

"Stranger, said the man escorting me, you are on the mercy of Hyperinor and the rest of the priests of Okria."

I smiled because the most unbelievable things happen in dreams.

"It's not a dream", said the one that was sitting higher than the rest, wearing a golden cloth, as if he was reading my mind.

"If you still haven't understood where you are", said one of the seven, "you are in the kingdom of Okria and you are at our disposal. We can decide about your life."

"But I haven't done anything", I replied in a trembling voice realizing that something was going wrong.

"The fact that you entered this kingdom illegally is a big mistake."

"But I didn't mean to enter", I replied.

"We'll look into that", said one of the seven.

Hyperinor pointed at one of the twelve who were sitting below the nine who immediately stood up and said:

"Stranger, you have to learn a few things…The kingdom of Okria is a kingdom of spirits. It is a closed community that remains like this since the old kingdoms died. Nobody leaves and nobody comes. We've been the same for centuries. We have chosen this place because it has the ideal universal currents but mainly because we have been connected to it since our existence with bonds that go beyond human standards.

We have the power to control a large part of the creatures that exist in the invisible world not only only on this island but in the area around. Our six Priests-Mystics, having as a leader the great Mystic Hyperinor, whose descent is lost somewhere in time, are our biggest hope in the battle between the Good and the Bad under the protection of Agitora Apollo.

This symbolic group of seven holds the Earth and vibrates in the seven colors of the rainbow, the seven music notes, and the seven planets. Every Priest-Mystic represents one metal and rules the powers.

I begin with the Supreme Hyperinor. He is represented by gold which is the only metal that lasts in time and its glow never fades. He rules the power of the invisible and he expresses creativity and thinking. His profound insight enables him to be in many places at the same time, control, supervise and create for the Good.

Porfirion, is the Priest-Mystic who is represented by copper and rules the fire.

Ietion, is represented by silver and rules the water.

Ixion, is represented by zinc and rules the air.

Melas, is represented by iron and rules the numbers.

Krantor, is represented by lead and rules the time.

Ioxos, is represented by tin and rules the colors. Nothing is impossible for them."

After the end of this presentation there was silence in the room. Everyone was looking at me with a thorough look. I turned to look at the symbol I was holding in my hand but all I saw was my fist. There was nothing else.

Hyperinor nodded and immediately one of the nine said: "When somebody comes here, they never leave."

As soon as I heard that for a second time I realized how unlucky I was and that gave me the creeps. I felt something turning in my stomach and my breath became faster. My legs were trembling and I wasn't sure if I could stay up for a longer time. I felt a sob in my throat and I tried hard not to make it show in front of them. I am strong I said to myself, I am strong.

"The symbol of Okria you found, represents god Apollo, gold represents our master Hyperinor with six other metals around him which represent each one of us."

"In the visible world it has the ability to last seven days, one for each metal. The gold remains on the seventh day and then it dissolves and disappears."

"In the spiritual world our symbol is in the form of the air. It is not real. Once every 100 years, though, one of our heroes takes on a mission in the real world unless there is something else more urgent in the meantime. In this case the metals that are in selected places of the island have to transform after our heroes have taken them.

This demands courage but mostly it requires the power of thought and will from the one who will dare to do it. Only our heroes are able to carry out this mission. But there are the evil powers which don't want the Good to win and they place obstacles making it hard for our heroes to carry out their trials with the aim to send them to Chaos, which they sometimes achieve.

They are devious and use whatever it takes. The guy you met at the shepherd's house was one of ours who didn't manage to come back. He is the only one who wasn't a hero and was sent to a mission, but the evil powers with Nohra as master managed to take him out of the mission and send him to Chaos."

"The symbol of Okria he was holding slipped from his hands and that gave them the chance to attack him. It was the seventh day of the mission in the real world and after that he would return. You caught the last metal, the gold, before being dissolved, that's why you came to our world as soon as you did that. Since our society is really closed, now that one of ours has left you will take his position."

"You will be one of us."

"But why me?" I cried. "Why did this happen to me?"

"Because you have no relatives to cry for you, neither friends to look for you", said one of the seven.

"I want to return", I said and my sobs shook my body. "I want to go back", I cried again.

"It's impossible", replied one of the seven. "But even if there was one possibility you still couldn't make it."

"I will make it", I shouted eagerly. "I will make it."

It seems I screamed it out loud and everyone looked at me ironically, smiling and commenting.

"Only our heroes achieve that and you are nothing but a frightened child who is shaking."

"I will try", I screamed, without being so sure this time.

"Do you mean that you can go through the trials like our heroes?"

"I want to try."

There was laughter in the room as if I had told a joke.

"It's not just the trials. You will have to confront Okria's enemies as well."

"The demons of abyss are lurking. The underground spirits are looking for a victim and the servants of the evil criminals and monsters are searching for food and prey desperately."

"The old dark powers of Mithra who fight what's sacred for us in order to impose their own laws and the ancient fights that have been taking place since the beginning of the humankind continue - they are still here. They change form and name depending on the time and place, but they are the same deep inside."

"Cruel and bloodthirsty, they use all their means to achieve what they want which is to impose their dominance. Do you think you can make it?"

"I will try", I said, running out of breath.

"If you fail, you will not have another possibility to try again, if of course you survive through all the dangers."

I shook my head. I didn't even want to think of this possibility.

"Your biggest enemy is yourself, said one of the seven. He will fight you and diminish all your attempts. Because the evil and the good both exist inside us. All the fights take place there, firstly. When the good prevails we live in harmony with clear consciousness, but when the evil prevails we commit the worst things. Worse than what the powers of the evil would do. So ask yourself if he can do it. This is your last chance. After answering that there is no return."

My mind stopped. Who and what could ask? I wasn't even sure of what I wanted. I couldn't think logically anymore. All I could think of was the fear I was feeling for what the future was holding. I was about to do either the most stupid thing in my life or the biggest achievement. Provided of course, that there was logic in all this.

I nodded my head to meditate and look at what was happening inside me.

"Ok", I heard from a higher place. "Since your answer is positive let the procedure begin."

I tried to scream, to say that I nodded my head in order to think not to show that I was accepting to fulfill the mission, but the people started leaving and the noise they produced covered my protesting. But if had the chance what would I actually say? Nothing more than the acceptance of the trials? Unless I had decided to stay in the strange world of Okria forever.

At least, I will try, I thought to myself. I was imagining the heroes and that place to be different. I was probably looking at only the good side in my fantasy and I was discovering now that the difficulties and dangers are many and for every action to achieve a good aim one must undergo hard trials. I looked high at Hyperinor while the room was becoming empty and I noticed his cruel look changing. He was rather looking at me with compassion as if he were looking at someone who was dying. I avoided his look and stood there feeling embarrassed as nobody was paying attention to me.

Where will I go now? What will I do? What is waiting for me? There was silence in the room as everyone had returned to their places again. Hyperinor began to talk.

"God", he said, "is the infinity, the eternity, powerful will, creativity and love. Everything is love and attraction. The whole universe is motivated by this power. The power of opposites' attraction. Love is the triumph of life. It beats death. Love is the oldest of all the other gods, according to the Mystics, and holds the key of all living creatures. Love leads the heroes from the depth of Chaos to the top of Heaven. It is the one that urges them to do the most incredible achievements and motivates them to become supermen. Your love for the earth - your island is stronger than your fear", he said to me. "He puts words in your mouth and arms you. You have made your choice. Accept the result."

He was silent for a minute but then went on talking.

"One of our heroes will show you what you want to see. The priestess of Apollo's temple, virgin Asteria will follow and control you. She will also be your personal trial."

When he finished talking, one of the twelve came close to me.

"I am Aetion", he said, "and I have been ordered to explain to you and show you the places and the trials you will carry out. But first they told me to take you to get to know the world of Okria."

We got out of the room, walked along the corridor when the well-known voice was heard again and something pulled my hand.

"He is mine. Let him", said the voice.

"He has got the mission", replied the hero.

"Can't you see that he won't be able to make it", said the voice, and I felt the pulling to my hand even stronger.

"Who is this who can be heard but can't be seen", I asked Aetion in fright.

"He is one of the demons of the Nohra Order."

"You won't achieve anything no matter how hard you try", said the voice sarcastically. "You will come to Chaos with us, you belong there."

I pulled my hand with force to free myself from my contender who did his best to discourage me. Aetion began to whisper incomprehensible words, like during an exorcism, and the voice of the demon of Chaos began to faint eventually.

We climbed up the steps through cave-like corridors. We passed many doors and we finally reached the ancient settlement of Okria. Everything was at their place like it used to be without ruins and debris and the people went on working; creating as they did before. I had many questions so I asked Aetion to explain to me.

"Why were all these spirits gathered in this place? Was it because it had the ideal universal currents as it was heard? For the priests I could explain it but for the simple people?"

"All these people, like me, really loved Okria, our land, when we lived in the real world", he said. "Can you see the steep rocks that protect it? Well, despite them, pirates from the East climbed up them with ropes working all night. The strong winds helped them not to be heard. Their leaders were the demons of Chaos that wanted to wipe out the temples of Apollo and shut the mouths of their Priests."

"They killed everyone at the settlement except for the Priest of Apollo who had strong powers and could vanish and appear elsewhere. But he asked with his own will to pass away and connect with all of us as our souls had flown."

"When passion and love dominate a soul like Mystic Hyperinor said, then this soul returns to the places it loved feeling happy to be there. So we all lived together in Okria loving each other, being really close, loving our land feeling a strong attraction to the rocks which are more than the ground. We remained spirits as we had asked from god because everything was positive to continue what we were doing in the kingdom and the life we had left then. The only thing we don't feel is hunger and thirst."

"The Priest of Apollo", Aetion continued, "acquired great strength as a spirit and unlimited power which God had given him. He became so powerful and renowned that he could control all the spirits of the island and out of it."

"Then the other Priests, spirits of Apollo, came from the old kingdoms to meet the Priest of Okria. Charmed by his power and strength on the invisible world they asked for permission to stay here creating the group of seven with the powerful thinking and influence. They taught how to process the metals each one represents."

"Hyperinor is the Priest of Apollo, right?"

"Yes", he replied.

We were now walking among a few houses of the settlement and I couldn't get enough of looking at and recording in my memory the ancient life as it used to be. We met a few who were carrying big pots while a little child was playing with a metal 'tserki' - a wreath.

Two women were knitting and a third one was weaving a white textile. A street prophet was giving a speech in the square talking about the battle between the good and the bad and some small children were playing; distracting the people from hearing the street prophet.

"All of them were killed in one day by the pirates?" I asked again with curiosity.

"Yes, all of us. The massacre took place long before dawn and we were sleeping."

That moment the prophet raised his voice and hand and said:

"The noise of the guns and the groans of the moribund and the wounded will be heard again. Darkness will fall on the Earth, which will be crawling in a filthy quicksand full of lies, slanders, pillages, crimes and greediness for gold. What the strong desires will beat justice."

These words remind me of something, I thought. We moved a bit more and stopped in front of a door. Aetion pushed it and we got in. It was a small room with a table, two chairs and wooden bed. This was all the furniture there. There were clothes on the table.

"Change your clothes and wear these that are on the table and give me yours. This is Hyperinor's command."

I hesitated for a while but Aetion's look wouldn't accept 'No' as an answer. I did what he told me reluctantly and gave him my clothes.

"Sit down and have a rest", he told me before closing the door. "Hyperinor will be waiting for you tomorrow to give you directions for the mission you have taken on."

I sat at the corner of the bed and started thinking. What is happening to me? Is it an extended dream for a reality I can't believe? I couldn't explain it. I let my eyelids close because of my tiredness even though my logic was trying the opposite, and I surrendered to Morpheas.

Chapter 11

The knocking on the door made me get up. I looked at my watch without thinking. Its hands were going left like crazy. I wondered. In the meantime the knocking on the door persisted so I stood up in great difficulty and opened it. Aetion was standing outside.

"Let's go", he said without specifying where exactly.

I turned to look at the room for the last time. What was the future holding? What surprises were waiting for me? Unknown. I felt I was walking on a thin rope. I took a deep breath - I did that very often - as if I was about to dive, and shut the door behind me.

It was indeed a dive into something frightening and unknown; that just the thought of it frightened me and made my flesh crawl. Where was I going? Lost in a lost world without being able to predict what would happen next. Was it a bad dream from which I would wake up one day or would I stay in the world of spirits forever? I looked around as if I was searching for help.

"Let's go", said Aetion reminding me that I was on death row.

I was walking beside him hesitantly along Okria's streets. I noticed that Aetion wasn't dressed the way he was the day before at the room. His robe was very simple like the one ordinary residents of Okria wore.

A load of pine tree trunks passed us by on a small cart which was being pulled by two men. One of them was from the group of twelve.

"Isn't he one of the twelve?" I asked.

Aetion smiled at me without answering. We met a child who was sitting next to a tiler trying to imitate his technique. Suddenly he turned to show his technique to the boy and to my surprise I realized that he looked exactly alike Hyperinor.

"But…isn't he Hyperinor?" I asked.

"Maybe", replied Aetion.

Hyperinor, it was certainly him, gave me a look full of mystery and went on with his teaching.

"Let's go", said Aetion.

"But weren't we going to Hyperinor?" I asked.

"Of course. That's where we're going."

I was wondering where. We had just walked past him. What are they trying to do? Drive me crazy? We arrived at a road where a house was being built. The stone craftsmen were working feverishly and among them I recognised again one of the nine. The one was was giving instructions to the builders had climbed up on a scaffolding inspecting the cornering of a stone. He turned and looked at us and I felt my heart beating like crazy.

It's impossible, I thought. We had left him helping a child learn the craft of pottery, how can he be at another post now? Unbelievable. I didn't have to ask now. I was sure that on our way we would meet Hyperinor again on different duties and another mission.

We left Okria behind and walked among tall pine trees. We got out of the forest and the ground became steep and rocky. We were climbing up in difficulty when we came across some steps some of which were carved on the rocks and other were built. It looked majestic on the horizon with its strong fortification, like a fortress.

All the time we thought we were getting there but we were still at the same place. We finally arrived and climbed up the stairs. The symbol of Okria was carved outside the door which opened on its own and we got in.

A big tiled yard was around the temple which was elevated on a pedestal. It seemed that there were rooms downstairs and there were stairs leading up to a part of the house with no windows except for the door.

We had been waiting outside for quite some time without moving when suddenly the door opened and we went in. There was a small hall and then a second door which was open.

We got in and I looked at Hyperinor who was meditating in a floating position. His look was distant and so was his mind. He was certainly dealing with other things besides us. We stayed there standing, waiting for some time, until he changed position and landed near us.

He looked at me and I felt as if he were taking all my inside world with his hand examining it with a microscope. I had nothing to hide from him. He saw my fears, my secret desires and thoughts, my thirst to return, even though I myself didn't believe I could make it.

It was dark when we got to the temple, as far as I could understand. The roof of the temple was a bit elevated from the building and was supported by small columns between which there were gaps serving as windows. Through them I discerned the stars. Aetion left and I was alone with Hyperinor. I didn't know how to act. I was trying not to look at him in his eyes.

"I could tell and show you a lot. I could tell and show you not, on the other hand. This is your wish and choice", he said slowly.

I had to answer but I didn't know what. What could he show me? Did it have to do with me, the spirits, the trials? Whatever it was it would certainly scare me. On the other hand, not knowing was worse than knowing.

"I want to know." The words slipped from my mouth and at the same time I regretted uttering them although they were true and required courage to tell them which I didn't know I had.

He looked at me in my eyes with an expression of pity for me, the same he had in the room the other day.

"Follow me", he said and walked towards the door.

I ran behind him in fright and curiosity. At the back of the temple there were stairs that led to the roof. We climbed up and he stood still reciting with his eyes closed:

"The one and only, the triform triangle, that repeats itself, adds and subtracts it, runs the universe. Past, present, future. Mind, will, creativity. Centre, ray, periphery.

The law of the universe which conditions everything is based on these numbers. Remember and store in your mind. 1 and 3".

There was silence after what Hyperinor said, and I was trying to absorb everything like a sponge, to understand and keep in my mind as much as I could.

"Fortunately the evil exists", he said and after that there was silence and I began to feel puzzled. "Fortunately the evil exists, he repeated, so that the good can be seen and highlighted. Without the evil, the good would be worthless".

His last statement brought me back. Since I had been making up stories in which the good triumphs over the evil, how could I be for the opposite side?

"Nothing is correct unless you interpret it from all aspects'', he said and after a few-minute silence he opened his eyes.

"Touch my hand", he said but I didn't dare to do so. "Touch my hand", he repeated, and close your eyes.

I reached out my hand hesitantly and felt something like electric power penetrating me. I closed my eyes and then I began to see all the difficulties of the tests I was going to go through and I started screaming with fear like a wild animal.

Monsters with lots of tentacles were hissing and crawling menacingly from the earth's depths. Steep tops of mountains that I had to climb up and down, to balance and jump. Depths of seas and demonic monsters with deformed bodies I had to fight with.

Bodiless demons with penetrating voices were coming to my ears and made me feel disappointed in what I was about to do.

Demons of the air the size of big clouds with forms that were constantly changing, were coming menacingly towards me while a devilish air was whipping my whole body making it hurt and seeking salvation in death. Gorges in deathly silence and me moving in blindness to their bottom, to darkness like a mole, while demons from both banks were throwing stones at me in order to extinguish me and make me disappear.

There were storms in my mind bearing doubts about what's good and what's evil and which way to follow. Fleshly desire provoking you, making you lose your way, aim and control. Figures of good spirits which are willing to help you but in the end it is proved that they are demons of darkness wearing the robe of kindness.

Figures of beloved people are called forth to convince you that you can do the impossible. All demons, who play with your emotions having the appearance of your beloved people ,cry out loud, call upon love bonds, scream your name to move you. I don't know who to believe.

"You are not going to make it", they shout from everywhere. "You are not going to make it. You are so small, petty, a worm compared to us. There is no other choice for you but not to try at all. If you try, though, it's better for us. We'll take you with us to Chaos. So try it. Try, hero! Let's see your endurance. Try it so that we will keep you with us forever''.

Other voices appear repeating the same, and laughters of bodiless demons are deafening me.

"If you want to become a hero, you have to try", screamed some.

"Why try at all since you are going to fail", replied others.

"Whatever you decide you are lost", screamed all together.

"Be a hero! Be a hero!"

"You are ours. You are ours."

I started screaming together with them with my body trembling as if it was struck by electric power. I felt as if I was holding a pneumatic drill in my hands out of control.

"Calm down", I heard someone saying, and I opened my eyes.

My body was still trembling as if I were naked in the North Pole, and my nose, mouth and eyes were extremely wet. I kept on screaming even after he had touched me on my shoulder.

"Calm down", he said.

I wiped away my tears. I felt naked in front of him. Nothing. Zero. Worthless, pointless, empty. I had forgotten my bombastic statements of me becoming a hero. Now I understand why they looked ironically at me in the big room. Now I understand why they laughed at me when I said that I wanted to try.

They knew better. I didn't imagine that there would be so many hardships and such insurmountable obstacles; beyond human limits. Where was I going? What was I trying to do?

"Can you do it?" There came the relentless question of Hyperinor who had been standing quiet for long, waiting for me to come round from the shock I was in.

Probably not. I won't make it. I would have been better off staying in Okria like a spirit, rather than end up in Chaos with the demons. I searched my soul to find even a speck of matter that would object to my decision, but I was sure. Something inside me like a small spark flashed. I looked again. Nothing. I uttered my decision.

"I will try." It was heard but it wasn't me who said it.

"I am your consciousness, you idiot. I said it", I heard inside me. "Can you put up with your destiny without fighting it? Can you bear to reconsider your ideas and beliefs? Only the petty, the beggarly, those who are worthless and are easily influenced make these decisions because they are forced by the fear of the unknown and failure, they are not consistent and refuse to fight. Nothing is impossible for people".

I raised my look on Hyperinor. He looked at me in sympathy and said:

"Just the fact that you saw what you are about to go through and maybe more, and still you resisted your fears and dilemmas and said you will try it, is a sign of a hero. But you are still in the beginning. You haven't even started. You may flinch just before the end. But even then you have the right to abandon it all."

He put his hand on my shoulder and we stood at the corner of the roof. He closed his eyes, as if he was praying secretly, and suddenly something lifted me. We started rising up and I was so scared that I didn't even move for fear of falling down. We stood at a small distance from the temple and were floating.

With a movement of his hand the crust of the Earth became transparent as if it was made of glass and various creatures appeared. Creatures of the air and the Earth began to form underground moving like microorganisms in a microscope. Blind, slimy creatures with many tentacles were looking for their food in the dark. They were in caves some lurking and growling and others competing to death in order to assert themselves and rule their region.

Ancestors of the Titans, huge and appalling, guard the Earth and with their tremendous power push enormous rocks from the slopes against their victims and the thunderous noise they cause, echoes to the gorges. Elves of the torrents, of the forest, the water and sea. Elves of the fire, the air. They were so many that I couldn't record them in my mind. Dryades, Amadyades, Niriides, Oceanides, Limoniades, Meliades, Esperides. I heard Hyperinor enumerating them.

I was looking again and again discovering new ones each time. I was looking at these unprecedented creatures in ecstasy, full of admiration and I couldn't imagine that they really existed even though I had heard the names of some. We flew to the sea and then other ones even more bizarre appeared. Some of them had fins, others not. Some were long others had antennas, bright knobs, opalesce flakes in silver, gold color, fluorescent. I didn't know which were good and which were bad. I'm sure there were both of them. After he had showed me the invisible world we landed in front of the temple's entrance. He said:

> "It's worth fighting for the Good even if he thinks he won't make it. You fought inside you, you had your first battle and won. Even bigger are waiting for you. The Evil is

everywhere, even inside us. The balance between the visible and invisible world is achieved with continuous battles. Small and big ones."

The stars were shining and we were in the middle of the night. Aetion appeared and I was about to follow him. Then, Hyperinor opened his arms and with cyclical movements as if he was holding an invisible sphere which he was squeezing to make it smaller, he kept on for a few minutes. Inside his palms appeared small electric holes until the invisible sphere shrank into his two hands. When he opened them again a small fluorescent blue sphere kept floating.

"Take it", he told me. "You may need it some day. But I want you to be careful. The more you ask for its help the harder the tests will get because of all that it will offer you."

It's pointless, I thought. But you never know. I may need help and I will then have to think seriously of whether I will use it or not. I reached out my hand hesitantly to touch it, and my fingers began to feel numb. I moved a step behind and the small blue sphere followed me. I thanked Hyperinor for the present and set off my returning together with Aetion.

I wasn't sure of how my night would be in the room. But if I judged from all the scary, remarkable things I had seen here in the temple one thing was sure. It would be full of nightmares when I had my eyes closed. Even if I wanted to sleep, it wouldn't be easy with everything I had been through that day.

I will reminisce my beloved, my childhood years to dissipate the nightmares. I remembered the girl that was playing near me many times when I went to the small beach of Marathounda. She would always ask to play with me and I would ignore her each time.

Engrossed in my daydreaming, I turned to look at Astradeni, that was her name, as if I wanted to tell her that it would be difficult to explain to her how I was thinking, that she wouldn't understand. But she kept on coming and sitting silently next to me gazing at the sea.

Chapter 12

I couldn't get any sleep to rest my tired arms and legs. I was terribly worried. The blue sphere was always there above my shoulder and I decided to go out for a walk. I got up and opened the door and in attempt to make the sphere stop following me, I made the move Hyperinor showed, a cycle around it, and it stayed where it was.

Aetion told me that the sphere was related to the positive magnetic field and so on, but I didn't understand very well how it had been formed and what power it had. Maybe he didn't give the explanations I had asked. There was no one at the street, everything seemed deserted.

I reached the edge of the city and climbed on a hill to take a view of it from above.

No sooner had I turned my head to look around, than I saw Aetion coming. I thought that he was probably looking for me. He came close to me and asked me to follow him. I asked him where we were going but I got no reply. It was probably something urgent.

We went quite far away and got onto a cave full of labyrinths. We passed a door and then another and in the meantime we could hear voices from the left and right without being able to understand where they were coming from and what they were exactly.

We opened another door and some creatures I had already seen during my insight through Hyperinor welcomed us. They followed us and we got into a big room inside the cave. Inside the room there was a strange guy standing, who smiled as soon as he saw me. His black hair fell in front of his two penetrating eyes which gave me a piercing look.

On his one hand he was holding a kind of scepter which looked like a stick wreathed in vine leaves, hitting it on the palm of the other. He was wearing a long dark green robe and strange creatures having the color of the host gathered around him forming a circle. Most of them had protuberant eyes like those of the fish that live in the dark, at the bottom of the sea.

"So it is you," said the strange guy in a deep voice. "You are the one who wants to act as if he were a hero," he added. I looked around searching for Aetion but he was nowhere, he had disappeared. I began to suspect that something was going wrong. Aetion was probably not on our side, or maybe he was playing two parts.

"I had a long journey to meet you in this cave," he added. "You should feel honored that I came to you and not you to me. And if you are wondering who is talking to you right now, listen to this:

> I am the night in a day, your secret thoughts, your unfulfilled desires, the unknown in the known, the anger in serenity, the thunder in the night, the negative in the positive, the other pole, the action in inertia, the movement in immobility, the sorrow in joy, the pain in happiness, the separation in love, the death in life. I am every opposite element, the opposite of opposites."

There was silence for a while. "What can I do?" He asked himself, in a hypothetical question that I would make to him. He continued by saying, "what the others can't do. I welcomed you in a simple cave which could be turned into a palace if I wanted to." And saying this he held his head with his both hands for a minute and then reached them out suddenly.

To my big surprise, the cave began to change, becoming a luxurious room with a throne, a richly decorated ceiling from which lit up chandeliers were hanging and it was full of courtiers dressed in fancy, colorful clothes with gems on them while at one corner of the room an orchestra was playing music. At that scene, a man was sitting on the throne with some jesters doing acrobatics and funny grimaces.

Everyone was looking at me because I hadn't changed and I was a new subject of study. Suddenly everything was quiet. He stood up from his throne and said, "we will return to the first image because I want you to understand that I am simple and I've come to speak to you on friendly terms."

And saying this he clapped his hands and the cave returned to what it looked like at first. I was left with my mouth open in surprise and admiration for what was taking place beyond my eyes.

"I know you are curious to find out who I am," he said. "My minions will tell you that," pointing at the various creatures that were following him. Nohra! Nohra! Nohra!, was heard in rhythm.

"Everything is symbolic in this invisible world. There is even a special pronunciation for the names as well," he said.

So that was Nohra, who was exalted for his power by the bodiless demon. I remembered Hyperinor and his phrase, 'nothing is correct if you don't interpret all its aspects'. I unconsciously started playing with his name, changing the tonality to 'a' or making anagram from the word. Suddenly while reading it backwards, I realized its secret meaning. NOHRA=ARHON

"I don't want you to take part in this mission," he said, interrupting my track of thoughts. "Every time their symbol is created, they acquire more influence and become more dangerous. Without their symbol at the moment," he went on, "they will be an easy prey for me to kill them and send them to Chaos. This damned community of Okria can't keep obstructing the plans of my empire all the time.

They basically can't make their symbol which they need, because through it they get power from Apollo and send you. If you don't make it, they have nothing to lose. They send you to Chaos.

If you feel you have made a wrong estimation or they have told you that they're the good ones and I am the bad guy, you are disillusioned. They have lied to you. What is Good is a personal matter for each person. Good is what is liked by each one of us. And I'm here to help you with that, to get what you desire."

Now how about that, I thought to myself. He will make me reconsider. He has got power, good intentions, what if he is right?

"If you cancel this mission," he said, "I will give you a large part of my invisible empire to govern because whatever happens you will stay in the world of spirits. That way you will escape being sent to Chaos and you will acquire dignity. But if you refuse to co-operate with me I will be relentless. I will chase you everywhere. You will suffer. You will beg to go to Chaos faster to find salvation.

So, what is your answer?"

"I need time to think," I said hesitantly.

He replied, "there is no time here. There is no point. Decide now!"

"I have given my word," I said terrified.

To which he said, "ha, ha, ha! There are no promises that can't be broken. So?"

"So..." I repeated, and was left without knowing what to do.

He hit the ground with his scepter and a muffled roar was heard from its depths. In a while, the ground of the cave opened at one part beyond my surprised eyes and an armed warrior began emerging while you could hear roars all around. The cave was shaking from the tremendous noise and when he was fully revealed he could reach its roof.

He had the height of at least five people and the metal laminates of his armor were shining as if they were hit by the sun. As if he hadn't just emerged from Earth. Even the monster-like creatures were shrunk at a corner being scared at the sight of that giant.

I couldn't utter a word and I was trembling waiting to see what would happen next. He lifted his foot and hit the ground and it felt as if an earthquake had happened. Rocks were falling from the roof and the walls of the cave. He walked towards me and lifted his leg above my head.

"Oh my God," I said, "my time has come. This human-looking monster will squeeze me." I closed my eyes and waited crying silently. Nohra's voice was heard and the gigantic warrior touched the ground slightly. He leaned towards me and saw his huge eyes throwing flames.

I was thrown like a dry leaf to the opposite wall of the cave as if I had been hit by lightning. My bones were hurting me and my head felt as if it would split in two. They lifted me up to stand on my feet and my head felt like a bell after a big hit. My entire brain and pulse were pounding like a hammer.

Nohra said to me smiling, "this is another example of my power and abilities. Now I will let the warrior leave to show you that I don't mean to push you." He clapped his hands and he began to decompose, until he finally turned into smoke that went up to the roof.

"So, what have you decided," he said more strictly.

"I want to try," I replied.

"To do what," he retorted.

"Watch what you say," the voice inside me said again. "Face it all as you want them to be in the societies you make up in your imagination. After all, he doesn't ask you to return to life. He says you will remain a spirit. He doesn't leave you room either - room or hope. Who knows? You may make it."

"To remake the symbol," I said and barely being heard.

An exclamation of disapproval was heard from all the monstrous creatures while Nohra's form was becoming frightening with eyes lying outside breathing fire and his body incurring from electrical discharges. Deafening rattlers were heard and the scenery of the cave began to disappear.

I was at the small hill that I had climbed to gaze the town while lightning was hitting the hill breaking the rocks around me turning the night into day. I fell down with my head on the ground and my hands over my head to protect myself from the uproar, the lightnings and thunder that were coming from all over.

"I had warned you," Nohra's voice was heard from a speaker. "There will be no mercy, while his loud laughter began to faint in the clap of thunder which also began to quiesce."

I started running back to Okria like a maniac as fast as I could. With my heart in my mouth I got into the small room and closed the door trembling with fear. I roosted in a corner like a hunted dog breathing fast. My heart was ready to burst as if it would escape from my chest.

I don't know how long I was standing at this position. When I regained consciousness I tried to organize my thoughts and I didn't feel like lying down and sleeping at all. I was very tensed and my mind was on the door In case I heard something. It would be dawn soon.

Chapter 13

I felt two hands lifting me trying to make me open my eyes. When they did open my eyes, I discerned Aetion staring at me and next to him there was another man. I must have fallen asleep at the corner of the floor.

"What happened to you," asked Aetion.

"You know," I replied ironically.

"I don't know anything and I don't understand. What do you mean." said Aetion.

"I saw you with them," I replied.

"With whom," he asked.

I quickly said, "with Nohra's submissives."

Aetion said, "You are wrong."

Angrily I said, "no, I'm not. Yesterday, you came and met me at the place outside the town that I had gone for a walk and asked me to follow you and then took me to them."

"It wasn't me. I can bring you four people to confirm that I was them last night," replied Aetion.

"Who was it then," I asked.

"It was probably one of Nohra's demons. They get the looks of one of us when they want to achieve something deceitfully," said Aetion.

I replied, "I didn't know what to believe. I couldn't trust anyone, anymore."

"Listen," said Aetion. "I have no reason to betray Okria, if that's what you think. I have given a great number of battles to protect its existence. Except for the sacred group of seven, we may not have great power to transform and affect situations but what we have is stubbornness and will, and every time we fight with these. If you don't trust me, I will tell Hyperinor to put someone else in my place."

"No, that's not what I meant," I replied a bit beggarly. Inside me though I couldn't help having my doubts.

"Sorry to interfere," spoke the one who was with Aetion. "Maybe I shouldn't enumerate what Aetion has done so far because it will seem that I'll be doing this because of our friendship and my wish to support him. It would be unfair to blame him, though."

"Evdoxos, I don't want you to support me," said Aetion interrupting him.

"Yes, but your great offer can't be overlooked," said Evdoxos.

Aetion replied, "stop flattering me Evdoxos."

Evdoxos then said, "no, I won't stop until I have made everyone aware of the fact that you had suggested and designed Amaxiti before we left the real world, which was a Herculean task. Difficult not only in conceiving it but also in creating it since it connected Okria with the port of Nanou giving us a connection to the sea.

It took three years to be completed, through gorges and steep slopes, giving impetus to the trade and the development of the settlement. A project regarded as the greatest development..."

"I told you to stop," interrupted Aetion grabbing his arm. "Enough."

I stood up and asked him why they had visited me...

Aetion replied, "today we are heading for the second Temple of Apollo where High Priestess Psamanthi will acquaint you with priestess Asteria, who will be present during your tests and will guide you to the places you have to go."

My bones were still hurting after many falls from the cave. Aetion and I got out of the town of Okria.

The other one who had come at first left to perform another mission. We walked through the forest and in a small glade full of cypresses was the Temple of Apollo. A woman in white was waiting for us at the entrance. She must have been about fifty years old.

"Welcome to the Temple of Agitoras Apollo," she said. "I am Psamanthi, the High Priestess of this temple, and I have been ordered to guide you to the Temple and introduce you priestess Asteria."

We got into the temple which was surrounded by rooms. Priestesses, dedicated to Apollo since they were born, were busy with various tasks for the temple. One of them must be Asteria, I thought. But which one?

Psamanthi took us to the sanctuary of Apollo and we stood in front of the god's statue, who tried to warn them at the night of the slaughter by the pirates by sending all the owls of the island to Okria. Even though the owls were croaking nonstop in order to wake everybody up, the wind that was blowing didn't allow them to be heard. It was the wind that the pirates took advantage of so that no one would take notice of them. She took us to the room where I was left speechless.

The whole room was full of women's hair. All the priestesses dedicate it to the temple from the day they are born till the day they die. He took one tuft which had white hair too. Psamanthi said "This is mine. From the remaining one," she said in sorrow and complaint. We returned to the Temple and Psamanthi went on her guiding.

"Can you see that crack on Apollo's statue", she asked. "It appeared one day before the slaughter and everyone thought it was a bad sign", she said. "Also, in the Temple of Apollo in Nimborio - as there are nine temples dedicated to Apollo on the island - all the small figurines, offerings to the god, had fallen and broken the day before and in the meantime the statue of the god at the Temple in Dafni shed tears. There were signs but no one could think that this tragedy would happen."

She then took us to an underground crypt after we had descended nine steps. There was a small room with a floor made of stones in the middle of which were two gigantic monoliths both of which had a circle carved on them. "These two ancient monoliths", she said, "are from the time of the first worshiping of god Apollo in Symi, thousands years ago. Those who can read the symbols say that one cycle represents the East and the other one the West, or that the one cycle is the Sun and the other the Moon."

The rain and the sun had affected them so greatly through all these thousands of years that unless they had these two cycles on them, one might think they were rocks transferred here from their natural habitat. After she had narrated us various miracles by the god Apollo, she led us in front of his statue again.

Aetion left in a nod of hers and I was left alone after she had asked me to wait for her to return and then she vanished into a nearby door. Looking at the statue of Apollo, his expression seemed strict at one time and when I was looking at it for a second time, I thought I could discern a smile on his face.

After a while Psamanthi got in followed by another priestess who wasn't older than eighteen. She brought her opposite me and I admired her sweet face with those beautiful eyes which looked like a sea at one time and a forest at another. She had long black hair and she was wearing a blue dress which matched the color of her eyes.

"This is Asteria," said Psamanthi. "She has committed herself with oaths before the god and all of us to follow and guide you throughout all your tests. She is not allowed to help you and she will remain pure as she has always been. Besides, as Mystic Hyperinor said, she will be your personal test. If you violate the rules, you will be severely punished. You will remain a spirit forever."

Psamanthi continued, "before each test you will come to the temple with Aetion in order to begin your mission together with Asteria. She is obedient, faithful to the commands and oaths she has given to Apollo, whom she has been serving since she was ten years old. Each one of us has their own secrets.

The secrets of the Temple, though, must be sealed in here. This is a rule which mustn't be disobeyed."

Then Psamanthi said, "you will give an oath before the god that you won't tell what you saw and heard here. So reach out your hand and touch the statue of the god and repeat after me - 'I swear to Apollo Agitor, the son of the Sun, that I will be punished to stay in the world of the spirits forever if I disobey my oaths.'"

After this procedure had ended, there was silence for a while and I looked secretly at priestess Asteria. This face seemed so familiar to me. As if I had met her somewhere. But I couldn't recall anything. Maybe it was just my imagination again.

"Go Asteria," said Psamanthi, and she left walking slowly, silent, distant and mysterious. I wondered what her character might be. Would I ever know or were the oaths she had given forbidding her to reveal her inner self? Who knows... We got out, and Aetion was waiting for us to set off our returning. We didn't exchange a single word until we reached our destination.

Chapter 14

THE VALLEY OF FIRE

I spent the whole night thinking about the first test I would undergo the following day. The tongue can convey the thoughts or the enthusiasm of the mind and heart at a particular moment, but when the body is tested through hardship the mind regrets many times what the tongue had dictated.

It was the eve of the big day and I was feeling ready to give it up; not being able to deal with the unknown that was expecting me. It was maybe because my stay here as a spirit seemed easier comparing to the fear of failure and my ending up in Chaos. The truth was I would set out unwillingly without having another choice.

While I was thinking about all these with my eyes closed, I was neither asleep nor awake with tiredness making my eyes close but with my mind not being able to calm down. I could hear every single noise but I didn't pay much attention to them.

The knocking on the door, though, made me get up. I opened the door hesitantly and saw Aetion waiting. "The time has come", he said prolonging my agony and anxiety.

It's one thing to make promises and another to fulfil them, I thought. I turned and looked behind at the room that accommodated me for so long; saying goodbye to it mentally and then closed the door behind me. Who knew if I would see it again. We left Okria and headed northwest.

As I could tell from our route we were heading again for the Temple of Agitor Apollo, from where we would get Asteria. Indeed, she was waiting for us at the Temple's entrance together with Psamanthi who welcomed us wishing us success for our difficult mission.

"May Apollo Agitor guide you as he guided our ancestors Dorians and they rooted in this land", she said. When we got out she greeted us and said, "my mission has ended. Asteria will take this place now." I tried to to utter a word but she stopped me. "I am aware of everything", she said, and nodded her head verifying his words.

Aetion headed for Okria and I turned to look at Asteria who had already set off going northwest without saying a single word. I ran to catch her and the truth is that I didn't like her manner. From her behavior I began to form an idea of her character.

She was snobbish, cold and distant probably because of her status which didn't allow her to talk to people but only to the gods. She could have asked me 'how I was' since she would be escorting me necessarily for a long time. Unless, this reaction of hers was due to her wish to keep me at a distance. So even though I wanted to ask her more details for my mission, her attitude didn't let me to do so.

All I could do was stare at her as she was climbing the rocky ground quick as a deer with her long hair waving. As I was looking at her I had this feeling again that I had seen her before. The route was tiring and long but she didn't utter a word. Though I wanted to understand her attitude, I left it for later. What mattered now was my own psychology which wasn't the best.

At a long distance I could discern a block of buildings surrounded by cypresses. Indeed we were heading there. When we arrived at the gate a priestess welcomed us and guided us inside. This Temple, as I figured out, might have been the second larger after the one of Miragetis Apollo where I had met Hyperinor.

Its gable was brown with round bas-relief depicting Apollo in its center. Down at the metope of the temple wrote: THARGILIO APOLLONI. The Priestess opened the gate and we entered. In the room, there was someone who looked like a Mystic from what he was wearing, at an invocation position praying in front of the god's statue with his back turned.

When he finished, he turned to us and I recognized that he was one mystic of the Sacred heptad that framed Hyperinor. They all took a bow, as I did. "This is Mystic Porfyrion", said the Priestess. "He will tell you the oracle for your mission, she added and left the room leaving us alone."

He got on a podium and looked at me thoroughly. I had the same feeling as the one back then with Hyperinor. He fixed his red robe, touched his white beard and leaned in the chair. Then with a serious, formal look he said, "the oracle is the following: 'At the valley of fire is the copper.'"

Where is this place? I wondered. But as it seemed I had heard what there was to hear. There were no explanations, no other statements because Porfyrion pointed at the bottom of the statue a small vase with a bung. Asteria took it to her hands and then showed us the door.

I got out unwillingly with a feeling of emptiness because of the uncertainty. The Priestess of the Temple was waiting for us outside and she told me, "take this vase because inside it you will bring the copper and hand it to Porfyrion again."

I took the vase from Asteria's hands. It was made of red pyrites and it was quite heavy. It was a work of art on which the craftsman must have dedicated quite some time to form it appropriately and carve on its one side the head of Apollo and on its other the symbol of Okria.

I stood outside the Temple indecisive without knowing where to turn to; but Etheria had already set off north so I ran behind her. Would I need anything? Did I have to dig to find the metal? What should I do anyway? No one gave me clear instructions.

I have to ask her, I thought again, when we reach the area as I was certain that Asteria was heading me to the Valley of Fire. Could she help me in any way? I had nothing else with me except for the leather bag Aetion had brought me. In order to hold it all the time, as he told me.

I suddenly remembered the small blue sphere Hyperinor had given me. I don't know if should use it after all I had heard. It was getting dark when the black rugged mountains began to appear behind the slope. We soon climbed a mountain which had no top as it seemed, with a slippery surface on which you couldn't discern individual rocks. Only then did I realize what surface it was.

It was lava which had become solid - we were climbing a volcano. I predicted that really soon we wouldn't be able to go further because it seemed impervious after a point even if we crawled. The area smelled of sulfur and we couldn't breathe easily.

I wondered how we would climb, if this was our goal, since after a point we would have to fly. We would make only if we were birds. I didn't even complete my thought when we turned right instead of going up as were doing till that moment.

After quite some time we reached a narrow opening as if a large piece had fallen from the top to that point. which looked like a corridor, forming a passage through which a person could barely pass. Asteria stopped outside for a minute when we arrived and I was curious to see how it was inside.

It seemed that the narrow passage kept on and then it was going up. I stopped and look back to see Asteria but she wasn't coming. I reached the beginning of the passage and I saw her waiting outside the entrance.

"Come", I said to her. She replied by shaking her head no. "Why?" I asked and regretted it immediately after my question. I felt so ashamed, and sorry for her when she made realize that her mission ended there and that the reason why she couldn't talk to me was that she was dumb!!!

I wanted to kneel and beg her to forgive me for all I had thought of her for all I had blamed her for about her character and manner. It wasn't my best moment and the sorrow I was feeling for that incident was added to the disappointment I felt. The truth was that if had seen it from another point of view, she wouldn't have been able to help me anyway.

I was hoping for Asteria to support me somehow. She would have been the only help I could have during those difficult moments, but now I realized that I had lost even that. Anyway. I shouldn't demand so much. Everything was completely unknown to me, so even just her presence was more than enough. I looked into her eyes asking her to forgive me deep inside and with a punch in the stomach I moved forward to the passage.

One could think that the side walls were about to squeeze me inside them as a clamp and make me disappear. I was zero. Nothing in a vastness which was asking to change the rotation of the Earth. A grain of sand that thought it had the power to resist and beat the immense ocean waves. I felt so tiny before the infinity!

I had moved forward a lot and the ground started being more downward until the Valley of the Fire, as Porfyrion named it, appeared before me in all its magnificence. I would call it Cursed Valley because it was a place that destroyed every hope of yours and filled you with fear and silence.

I reached the valley, a round area in red color with a tree in the middle. It impressed me so much that I couldn't explain it. A tree here? In the crater of a volcano? Indeed, it was a tree. A very big one actually.

It had got almost dark and I was heading to the center with the steep rocks surrounding me; taking strange forms giving the impression that they were watching and lurking me. It was a lunar landscape out of the world which gave you the creeps. A sick silence reigned. It was as if the sound of every step of mine was multiplying, echoing around the valley creating other sounds. Was it a natural coil audio or not?

I stopped and listened carefully. Nothing. I walked again and these sounds were heard again. I couldn't make out if it was the echo of my footsteps or something else. I was in a state of hyperstimulation with my nerves tensed and my ears open. Even a small sound surprised me and made me turn. The heat inside this place justified its name 'Valley Of Fire'.

The high temperature must have been coming from the depths of the Earth making the atmosphere unbearable and my skin pores shed all the liquids of my body. It was a natural vapour-bath that maintained and increased the temperature due to the height of the mountains around than enclosed the place.

I moved towards the tree, which from the long distance seemed to have leaves, too. It made me so curious that I wanted to see closely what kind of tree it was to grow in the middle of the cursed valley and could survive in this atmosphere where dead silence was omnipresent. How did it get moisture?

My feet were sinking in the red earth of the valley and I was feeling the heat immensely in the soles of my feet. A distance of less than fifty meters was left to reach the tree when suddenly a strong wind blew out of nowhere, creating a whirlwind around the tree.

I fell onto the ground prone to protect myself from the wind's fury and the dust it raised. It was so strong that removed the leaves from the trees and made them float in the sky. Soon, there was nothing left on its branches, which were left looking like hands raising, facing the sky in a supplication position.

When the wind finally stopped, the leaves paradoxically didn't fall to the ground but kept flying. I turned and looked at them in astonishment and then I realized that they weren't leaves but bats which were now turning over my head in a threatening way. Their intentions weren't friendly at all and I looked for something to defend myself. A branch of the tree was a few meters near me, I took it and started to turn it over my hand to repel them. They were moving about and screaming in a horrible way.

I hit one with the branch but unfortunately that turned it into a dog with the same features which was growling and showing me its teeth in a threatening way. So except for the sky I had gained another enemy on the ground which made me abandon my trying. I thought to escape but that was what the one who had sent these horrible creatures wanted. There was nothing left for me to do than stay still; waiting to see what they would do.

They were flying low, sitting on my head, my shoulders, my hands and my whole body until I was covered all over in these weird living 'leaves'. I felt disgust for these demons of the night which were hooked on me and brought me to my knees due to their weight; licking my body with their tongues. I was holding my breath so as not to scream, while that dog was barking around me.

Dressed in that weird robe, for how long would I be able to remain in that position? I tried to move a little but the bats grabbed me even tighter with their claws as soon as they sensed that I started moving.

Some of these disgusting creatures were sitting on my face, hanging from my ears, eyebrows and one of them was sitting on my nose looking at me with its appalling eyes as if it were mocking me. I tried to move again but their claws pierced my skin deeper from where they were hanging.

I could barely hold back a scream which was fighting to escape my chest. My feet were tired, trembling, and I was about to faint. I was hopeless, unable to do anything. My only reaction was expressed with sobbing and tears ran from my eyes and rolled on my cheeks. I blinked to keep my eyes open but I felt I had no more strength. I was about to fall on the ground.

I brought Asteria and her problem back to my mind. How much I needed her to help me! But except for the fact that she was far away she probably had taken an oath which she wouldn't want to break. Between the gaps that the bats' bodies were leaving in front of my eyes, my tears made my eyes blink and I thought I saw a shadow on the left. Something was coming unless it was only my imagination or my weakness.

A scream echoed and broke the silence and the bats flew high creating a sphere which was revolving around itself. In front of my astonished eyes they flew lower and formed a figure which was wearing a black tunic with a hood. It must have been a demon of the abyss from Nohra's order if not Nohra himself who had come to dissuade me from this mission, I thought.

"I know you are scared", he said, stopping opposite me in a voice that sounded as if it were coming from the depths of the Earth. "It's enough so far", he added. "If you move on, there is no return for you. It's still the beginning. Accept Nohra's offer and go back. The worst is yet to come." And with this last phrase he started dissolving and vanished.

I was left alone without being able to come around from the shock that the bats and demon's words had caused. Returning to Asteria without the metal would be the end. I sat undecided until I organized my thoughts and decide what I would do and then I noticed that the crests of the mountains and slopes seemed as if they were moving.

What on earth is going on? Do I have illusions? Is it possible? I wondered. In the dim moonlight even the ground was changing. Something was moving towards the centre where I was standing. Nohra will show his mania in another way, I thought. What is coming? What's that?

Looking very carefully I realized that the mountains moving against me were armies of weird creatures covering the whole valley coming towards me. I ran to the opposite direction but they were following me there, too. I moved back and tried to leave but I realized there was no way to escape. These creatures were coming from all directions.

What were my choices? Only one. The tree. I climbed up it as fast as I could because they were really close. I made it at the last minute. They surrounded the tree moving rhythmically screaming, "free us, free us." Their voice was so sharp that I closed my ears to try and escape, but in vain. The voices were not heard in my ears, but telepathically inside my mind.

The creatures were gray, thin and long with a height of about a metre. They were about as thick as my thigh and you couldn't distinguish their head from the rest of the body. It looked more like the head of an octopus. They had two slanted yellow eyes, two small hands with three fingers and small feet which looked like tentacles.

"Free us, free us", they were screaming and something strange was happening. The more time was passing, the louder was their voice and I couldn't bear hearing it. It was driving me crazy. I'm lucky they aren't climbing up the tree, I thought. No sooner had I thought about that, than they started gnawing the trunk of tree.

Whether I wanted it or not, I would land together with the tree in this frightening sea of creatures and the consequences were unknown. How can I free you, I screamed. Everything stopped immediately and there was silence. Nothing at all was heard.

Then I heard someone talking in my mind with a crying voice - "Nohra has condemned us to remain in this valley without being allowed to leave." I replied, "what prevents you from leaving"? Then I heard, "haven't you noticed that we don't have freedom of movement"? I hadn't noticed.

"Come down and see it for yourself", said the voice. To which I replied, "I'm not coming down because it's a trap." Then the voice said, "if we wanted to catch you, we could do it in an easier way, said the one that was talking on behalf of the rest. We could climb up the tree by using our hands."

He must be right, I thought, but still I was afraid to dare to go down. I climbed down cowardly until I reached the branches of the thick trunk and looked more closely. They were right. They were all wearing a collar around their neck connecting them with each other with a ring. They were divided in four groups, I assumed, as many as the points of the horizon in order to cover all directions.

But why had Nohra captured them against their will condemning them to stay in this cursed valley? I had barely finished my thought when the reply came immediately. They said, "we guard the valley so that no one will enter." Then I said "why, what is there in this valley and you have to guard it?" They said, "we'll tell you when you free us." "And how will I free you", I asked. "With a positive magnetic field", they said.

I remembered the sphere that Hyperinor had given me which must have been for that purpose. I said, "I haven't got the sphere with the positive magnetic field that would surely free you." The quickly replied, "try without it. If you really want it, it will happen." I went down with more courage and touched the ring with curiosity and hesitation to see how it really was. Nothing happened.

"Try again", the creature talked to my mind. I then touched the ring with my two hands and started to beg Apollo to help me find the solution. My fingertips began to get very hot and immediately after that, small blue flames came out of them causing a short-circuit and the creatures were freed right away.

I did the same with the rest of them and freed them all making them grunt happily. As soon as they were freed their gray color turned into white. They came close to me, stroking me, purring happily like cats do when they are pleased; showing me their gratitude. I asked them, "what secret does the valley hide"?

"At first", said the creature, "the valley wasn't like that. It was all green, full of grass, trees and animals. It was a small paradise. The tree in the middle is a sacred oak. When one day a hero from Okria came here on a mission, like you, looking for something he didn't know that Nohra's demons were watching him in order to prevent him from achieving his goal. But in that August afternoon, Amadryada, a nymph that lived in the sacred oak, saw the hero that the demons fought and ran after and decided to help him.

She tried to pull him in her trunk and hide him but the demons saw her and with Nohras's help, who wanted to take revenge for both of them, threw hot air and burnt everything. He changed the climate of the valley and made the volcano's fire start burning in the earth's depth. So the paradise that it once was, turned into hell. The nymph of the tree never appeared again and we guard the valley and notify Nohra if someone comes."

"Damned stranger", a frightening voice was heard. "You disobeyed my warning and freed the inferior creatures that guarded the valley. Prepare to feel my rage." With the finishing of his last words, a thump shook the ground violently and right away smoke started to come out of the earth.

"The volcano, the volcano" screamed the creatures in panic. "The volcano begins to activate", they said again, starting running here and there like crazy in order to leave the valley. The ground was shaking and started cracking and in the meantime the smoke became even thicker and the atmosphere was smelling of something that was being burnt.

Oh God! What am I going to do? I thought. Should I leave without the metal or wait for the lava that was about to jump out to kill me. I was lost anyway. Whatever I decided I was condemned.

I leaned towards a trunk of a tree and burst into tears. Why, dear God? Why? Why did I have to decide on which of the two ways I preferred to die of? Should I die now or later remaining a spirit forever? My tears rolled on the tree when suddenly I heard a soft voice of a woman calling me from the trunk inside.

"Help me, help me," said the voice. I bent down and listened carefully and the voice repeated asking for help. "Are you talking to me", I asked. "Help me", she said again. "I'm Amadryada, the nymph who lives in that tree. I had been waiting for so many years for a few drops to become alive again and you offered them to me with your tears. Free me." "How", I asked. The nymph replied, "carve a cycle on the trunk upon me."

How can I carve it, I wondered. I have nothing to carve it with. I searched for something hard though it was difficult to see clearly because of the thick smoke around. I touched something and hurried to bring to close and see what it was. It must have been a human bone of a unfortunate man who died in this cursed valley. It probably belonged to a lower body part, which had been broken violently in two, making a sharp tool looking like the ones Paleolithic cavemen used to have. Without wasting more time I returned to the trunk and carved a cycle with all the power I had and Amadryada got immediately out beyond me astonished eyes and took my hand.

"Thank you", she said, "but run. We have to make it." "I'm not coming", I said. "Come, before it's too late", she said. I replied, "for me it's late anyway. Either now or later."

"Save yourself", she insisted. I replied, "I can't save it. If I don't find what I'm looking for, I'm dead. So it's better to die here."

"And what are you looking for", she asked. I said, "the metal of copper which is hidden somewhere in that cursed valley." "I have it", she answered smiling.

"You? And where is it", I asked with curiosity and excitement. She replied, "I keep it in my roots all that time." "And how can we get it", I asked. She said "we have to pull down the tree."

I replied, "but we can't." To which, she said "when the soul of a tree comes out of it, it dies. It will remain alive for as long as I'm alive." In my panic and the rush of the moment, I didn't realize the horrible truth and the deeper meaning of her words. "What do you mean", I asked.

She said, "when the soul of the tree comes out, which is the nymph, the tree dies." "And the soul goes somewhere else", I asked. "No, they always die together", she replied. "That means that you will die", I said. She simply replied, "that's my destiny. Listen. If you want to take the metal and escape from the lava that's about to come out, you just have to rush."

I asked, "what should I do"? She simply replied, "you have to kill me."

"No, never", I screamed in horror. She said, "but I will die anyway soon. I'm just telling you to do it faster so that you'll manage to get out of here alive."

I said, "I can't. I don't have the strength to do such a thing."

"Then you condemn yourself", said the nymph. Why do they keep placing me in dilemmas? Why do I have to kill in order to save my life? "No", I screamed, "I won't do it", and hit the trunk with a punch.

The nymph said, "this bone that you are holding, she said showing it to me, belongs to the man who had come to the valley looking for the metal. I tried to save him, because the power of love has shaken me, but Nohra killed him. So it's logical, she said, stroking the bone as I was holding it, to die by a beloved person since I will die anyway." And while saying this she threw herself on the bone holding my hand pushing it into her heart.

I was shocked, speechless.

I saw her dying with horror on her face whispering, 'at the roots, at the roots'. I turned my head not being able to bear looking at what was happening. When I looked again, she had passed away with a serene look on her face. The tree immediately started falling apart. It was soon just a drift of earth as if someone had turned into sawdust and left it there.

I ran in a hurry and excitement digging the central part of the drift with my hands. My hands touched something hard and I pulled it out. It was a transparent sphere made of rock - which was probably quartz, I'm not sure - and inside it there was the metal. I put it in the leather where I was keeping the vase too and tried to orientate myself while small flames were coming out of the ground.

I couldn't see where I was going anymore so I set off blindy. I started running, looking at the moon that was covered by smoke and its light was dim, in order to remember where I had started from. As I was running flames were popping up in front of me blocking my way, making me change direction.

When I reached the end of the valley and the rocks began, I discovered that I had moved a lot more right from the opening of the passage, so I tried to catch up. I arrived at the passage and didn't look back as Lot did with Sodom and Gomorrah, because I could tell that the whole valley had turned into hell. Everything from the mountains seemed to have been in flames. I want to make it at least, I thought.

With all the power I had been left with I entered the passage, while the heat became more intense. I reached the place where Asteria was and found her terrified begging on her knees to God. She was surprised to see me. Maybe because she wasn't expecting me to be alive after the destruction that had taken place in the valley.

The smile she gave me brightened up her face and I screamed to her, "run to save ourselves, because the volcano is about to erupt." She didn't wait any longer. She stood up and started running. I didn't have enough power after my last effort I had made so Asteria stopped to wait for me many times.

We reached the foot of the mountain when the volcano began to erupt making a muffled hum. The valley seemed to have been covered in lava which overflew looking like a river up in flames. When we felt safe at last, I sat on a rock breathing fast. Asteria pushed me to show me that we had to go on because the lava was covering everything. I hadn't told her about the metal yet and she didn't know whether I had found it or not.

As soon as we escaped anger, I asked her to sit down for a little and I burst into tears. I was crying non-stop and she looked at me in wonder. I just couldn't keep inside me all this pressure I was feeling. I sobbed myself and didn't feel ashamed of it. I was crying more for the nymph who was sacrificed to save my life.

After I stopped crying and calmed down, she asked me with gestures why I had done this thinking, as I understood from the her look, that I hadn't found the metal of copper and I was empty-handed. I sat down and told her about my adventure in great detail and when I had to mention Amadrya's death again, and the way she died, I was in tears again.

Asteria was listening to me carefully and her facial expressions changed according to to my narration. Her contentment for the happy ending of my adventure was written on her face. As we were heading to the temple of Thargileio Apollo I went on telling her details I had forgotten on my first narration even though I had a bitter taste in my mouth and I was so thirsty.

With our chatting I didn't realize how we reached the temple, where they welcomed us at the gate with smiling faces knowing - I don't know how - the outcome of the test. At the room of the temple, Porfyrion was sitting at the familiar pedestal and took the sphere from my hands, which I had to break and carry the metal in the pot made of red obsidian. Asteria did it for me.

"We have got the first element", said Porfyrion. "You deserve to be called the 'Sun-bearing soldier'", talking to me. I was proud as a peacock with Mystic's words and left the room jumping with joy. When I got out I saw Aetion waiting for me to return to Okria. I searched for Asteria but in vain. She had disappeared. She probably had went to her own Temple.

On the way I couldn't get enough of narrating my experiences to Aetion this time. At night I couldn't get any sleep. The scenes of my adventure kept coming over and over again on my mind especially Amadrya's death. If it hadn't been for her, I wouldn't have made it. I would have returned empty-handed. Her sacrifice at the right time not only saved me but also brought a happy ending to my test. I thanked her again silently and fought with my thoughts before Morfeas (the god of dreams and sleep) came to me.

Chapter 15

As Aetion told me before leaving, I had three days to rest and for each test I had three days to try to carry it out. That was something. I would have the chance to try again if I didn't make it to find the metal on the first day.

I didn't do anything special on the two days. I was just sitting and thinking about various things like how I had got here, what I was trying to do, my first test on the crater of the volcano which ended successfully, nymph Amadryas, Asteria and so on. I was wondering whether my new tests would be hard and what I had to expect during the whole adventure. How would it end?

On the third day I decided to get out without going far away from Okria. I had learned my lesson well with Nohra. While I was passing by one street, an old man with a long beard was on a stone and on one minute he was making a speech and the next minute he was discussing with the people around him telling oracles and making prophecies. I stood for a while.

"Who is he", I asked someone beside me. "Zephxis Tephtlousios. Philosopher and prophet but also a heavy drinker too", replied the stranger next to me. He said the last words with a wide smile on his face. I mingled with those who were listening and when he saw me, he stopped the chat he had with somebody and began saying:

"When you see dust and fog, I will be dancing there with Apollo's rays stroking my body. Changing colors, yellow, white and orange on the burning stone by Apollo, like tongues of melted air, I will be praising him. At the desert of a gorge I will be the lonely bird, the snake that guards the ruins of the ancestors, a scream in the middle of the night."

Then he stared at me saying, "two of the four cardinal points define the worlds where the sons of the gods came to. At the fifth letter of the alphabet is the beginning and at the thirteenth the end". Then he stood opposite me and touched my hand.

He held it looking at me in the eyes for a few minutes as if he was feeling my pulse and added, "the fire of your thought will melt the matter just like the wood that eats it out." That old man is very weird, I thought, as he was setting my hand free going elsewhere.

Chapter 16

I woke up in the morning waiting for Aetion to come, but he didn't. Was I wrong or not? It was the day I had to go through my second test. What happened? Not having to do anything, I sat and waited but Aetion was nowhere. It must have been evening, the sun was setting when there was a knock on the door. I opened the door and it was him. "I've been waiting since morning", I said. Aetion replied, "this test will start at night with the full moon, like I have been told, that's why I came now."

We set off for the Temple of Agitor Apollo where we met Asteria with Psamanthi and after they had welcomed us we headed for the Temple where I would get the oracle from the second Priest Mystic. Everyone was silent. We headed south among cypresses and rocks until we saw the Temple near the sea.

There was tranquility at the harbor as the sun had just set and the evening was quite pleasant. The whole Temple estate was surrounded by a high wall which was protecting it mainly from the side by the sea. Next to the Temple there were olive trees and lentisks.

We got in and they were waiting for us and guided us to the chamber of the Temple. Aetion remained outside. The Mystic was dressed in a silver tunic and when we knocked on the door he was gazing at the sea from the window. A Priestess opened the door and said, "Mystic Yetion", and got out in a hurry.

We stayed there waiting for the oracle. Yetion smiled and said, "the fantasy is creative when it is accompanied and combined with values and ideals. You have made the first step, he added addressing to me. You are in the beginning."

Then there was silence and after a while he spoke again, "the oracle for the second test is the following - 'At the gorge of Nanou at the place where the rain has dug up the rock. In the Earth's depths, in the lap of water, is the metal.'"

Yetion revealed the pot which was at the feet of the statue of the god. Asteria took it. It was like the first one but made of a different material. If I wasn't mistaken, it must have been made of Rock Crystal. We got out and met Aetion. I turned back as we were leaving and noticed the name of the Temple. Evdomagetan Apolloni.

"I'll come with you for a while", he said, "because it's on my way, and I will leave afterwards." So, I had the chance to ask him to solve some of my queries during his stay with us.

"I had the impression", I said addressing to Aetion, "that the metals I had to bring were in a deposit underground and not in small quantities separately placed by some according to the Mystics' order. Why did that happen", I asked.

Aetion replied:

> "The reason, according to the Mystics who choose the places on the island each time, is that there are certain powers such as telluric currents, active magnetic fields, etc. which function and increase the ability and influence of the metals' elements giving them special qualities.

> These places where the metals are put, to put it in other words, are like junctions; pulses that beat in certain parts of the body because the most vital 'veins' of the island pass through them, vitalize and create the cosmic tides which influence the invisible world, and through it, the visible one as well.

> The same happens with the nine Temples which are dedicated to Apollo. They are located in places which had been chosen during the ancient times for having the same

qualities. These parts control, supervise, regulate and increase the vitalizing power sent by God and protect the island from the invisible evil powers. They are strong centers loaded with energy."

We walked quietly for a while among lentisks and I brought the oracle of Aetion back to my mind. When I heard him talking about the gorge of Nanou, that name woke up my childhood memories. I had associated Nanou with what my father had told me and to be honest it was the only place that caused me fear.

The reason was the story he narrated me many times about the Varvalakka of Nanou, as he was called. He was an undefined creature as far as his appearance is concerned, because it appeared in various forms always in order to frighten people and scare the animals of the area away. He made his presence noticeable by starting to throw huge rocks at the gorge or in the sea.

Most of his appearances were mentioned to have been taken place in the gorge so it must have been his favorite place. When I was told as a child about the boulders he threw from long distances into the sea, I would compare him in my fantasy to Cyclop Polyphemus who became blind by Odysseus and his comrades and was trying to make them sink in that way. But he didn't appear only in Nanou. He could do the same in Dysalona as well.

One of the stories about Varvalakka - whose name has probably come from the name Vrikolakas which means vampire - which I prefer, was the one that took place in Dysalonas by an uncle of mine who narrated his experience to my father. One day, when my uncle was eighteen years old - before he left for Australia - he left the harbor of Pedi with his brother and their uncle by the boat in order to catch garnfish. This kind of fish is usually caught with a fish spear or net.

The search of the surrounding area was fruitless until they arrived at the opening of the port of Dysalona. You must visit Dysalona. The stories don't do it justice. The awe, the fear and the admiration that this vertical mountain with its inaccessible mountains causes you. When you look at it closely you bow to nature and the majesty of the Creator.

The small chapel dedicated to Saint George the Dysalotos, makes your awe and admiration for the scenery even greater, especially when you compare its small size to the giant's feet which he has placed on the left and right as if he protects the place that got his name in that way. No man or animal has ever laid foot on its middle and most imposing vertical mountain, except for the eagles, and till the end of the world no one will ever do so.

My uncle Fotis, to return to our story, rowed right as his uncle ordered him in order to search for octopuses. The sea was calm, nothing was heard except for the sound of the oars when plunging into the sea. It was a difficult time to own an engine. So the sails and oars were part of the daily routine.

So when they finally reached the right part of the port looking for octopuses, a noise was heard like the blowing of the wind, and a huge rock landed next to the boat. This caused water to get into it and my uncle asked what it was. Nobody knew what to say, but my uncle was suspecting something so he ordered to go to the center of the port for security. After that, two similar gusts of wind landed two huge rocks on the left and right filling causing more water to go into the boat.

Seeing that things got worse, pale from fear with their hair standing on end, they didn't know where to go. Their uncle, with his eyes popped out from fear, couldn't think reasonably. How could the rocks find them even in the middle of the port?

In a hurry and without a logical explanation, he asked them to row out to reach the beach in order to save themselves because it was a miracle that the rocks hadn't destroyed the boat yet.

"Put the boat out on the beach so that we can get out to land", he shouted. My uncle, rowing with all his strength, headed for the beach. Unfortunately a bigger surprise was waiting for them. As they were reaching the beach, a strong wind blew and became a tornado uprooting the bushes and whatever was on its way. It was like a ball drifting everything.

When they saw that it was coming toward them, they tried desperately to avoid it but with no luck. It hit the boat on the side where the oar was and broke it. They were at its mercy. It could do anything it wanted to them…

They were trying to take the water out with one oar and a half, pushing the boat toward a narrow escape. They reached their destination in the early morning having lost half a life due to fear. So I had to try and carry out my second test at the den of this unpredictable, mysterious creature and I didn't know how it would show its intentions.

It would certainly not coax me but instead, it would show me who dominates and rules his area. In what form would it appear? To some shepherds he appeared as a huge caveman in the opening of a cave in Nanou which they call Scordallous.

I was wondering what experience should I expect. But it won't be only him. Nohra's demons won't miss the opportunity to dissuade me from my mission. I have always wanted to learn where the Varvalakkas of Nanou that haunts the area came from. Now I have the chance to ask Aetion.

I asked, "do you know anything about the creature of the gorge in Nanou?"

Aetion moved as if he was thinking about it and said:

> "The creature that haunted the gorge is said to be the reflection of god Mithras from Zoroastric religion which was first worshiped by the Chourrites in the ancient times. The pirates of Cilicia brought it here when they began their invasions. The birth of Mithra took place in a stone, as it is claimed, and since the beginning of humanity fights with Apollo. That's why he always appears at night to frighten those who worship the Sun."

There was silence for a while and then he added:

> "Nohra probably calls him from time to time, but it's not certain that you will meet him when you go to the gorge. I think certain factors should also concur to make it happen, such the filling of the Moon, the negative magnetic field and others.

> I haven't met him yet but the truth is that I haven't passed by that place at night. During the nine years I had been supervising the construction of Amaxites that goes up the gorge, I never had an unpleasant meeting. As I said, though, I have never been there at night."

We reached Okria settlement and Aetion greeted us at that point wishing us success. We started our descent at a steep slope which was making it even more difficult for us as we were moving. In the meantime the full moon started appearing from the East.

We reached Amaxites, which was designed and constructed by Aetion moved forward walkin on one part of it. I really admired its construction and the turnings on the steep mountain. It was a Herculean task. We left Amaxites and descended vertically.

We were at the most dangerous part of the gorge the Skali, as it was called. Once you descend, you can't return to the place you came from. Asteria stopped looking uncertain.

"Have we arrived", I asked.

She shrugged a shoulder as if she were saying that she didn't know. Next I asked, "where is the place which has been most corroded by rain?"

She made the same gesture again. I searched around the place and besides a natural shelter at the root on the left side of the gorge, there was nothing else. We were in a stone pit where the stream probably came down torrentially in the winter creating a waterfall.

Suddenly a baby's cry was heard on the right side of the gorge which was becoming louder and louder. I turned curious to look at Asteria who was also wondering. Then the voice changed, without stopping, into a woman's voice which was screaming at such a high pitch that it was deafening you and the echo from the gorge was making it even louder.

Together with the voice there was also noise coming from the stones that were shaping up on the gorge and at the same time before our astonished eyes with the sound of the voice being turned into a chant as if sung by an Asian monk, a gigantic creature was created which looked like a caveman . My blood froze while the voice continued being heard this time as a baby's crying again.

We were speechless beyond the weird, out of the Earth birth of that creature and what came to mind was the name of the Vavalakka of Nanou. His arriving was impressive and so was the voice that accompanied its birth. I tried to find an explanation for the changing in its voice and associate it with its birth.

What I came up with was that the baby's crying was the child being born, whose mother screams when she gives birth to it, and the monk's chanting blesses its birth. This was the explanation I gave to what I had seen. No sooner had I thought about this than my surprise turned into fear looking at what it was about to do.

The giant seized a huge rock and with a scream he lifted it over its head throwing it against us; making the gorge echo with the sound of the rocks being broken. Fortunately, the rock crashed a bit far from us so we escaped the inevitable. With this movement, though, I addressed to Asteria shouting, "under the hollow of the rock quickly!"

We both ran and stood under the shelter while the rocks were breaking before our eyes. The rocks kept being thrown and were accumulating in front of us and their pieces were scattered with force everywhere. The ground was shaking and the noise was deafening.

The throwing of the rocks continued and soon the pit was full and we were in danger of being buried alive in there. The moonlight had disappeared and there wasn't any hope from anywhere. It was impossible to move the rocks. There were just very narrow gaps between them and we couldn't pass through them and the dim moonlight was lighting our grave weakly.

I was desperate. I couldn't discern Asteria in the dark. I started looking for her when she nudged and pulled me to look at something. On the left at the corner of the shelter down on its root, there was a small gap through which one person could fit to pass. I hadn't noticed it yet with the fear of Varvalakkas and our agony to save ourselves.

This small gap was going through the rock and was the entrance of an underground tunnel or a cave with unknown direction. We entered it crawling but after a while we were able to stand on our feet. Where would this tunnel lead us to? It was so dark that we could understand what was in front of us and what we were stepping on only by touching it. After a while the ground became vertical and we could hear a hum which became louder and louder. When we got near we understood where it was coming from.

"It's an underground river", I said. I had just finished my sentence when I heard people talking and someone said, "why have you come to our world?" In the meantime, the torch was lit up.

The torch's fire was trembling and becoming stronger; helping discern the figure of the creature holding it. It was hairy. It looked like a human but had long hair all over its body that reached the ground and two round eyes; opening and closing them like a cat.

Other weird, sticky creatures with bulging eyes were forming a queue behind it. They looked as if they had just got out of the water so I thought that maybe they were creatures of the water. What should I do? We got in to get away from Varvalakkas and closed ourselves in this underground tunnel with no exit. I turned and looked at Asteria who was left behind looking terrified waiting for what would happen next.

"Don't move ahead", I told her, "stay where you are."

The worst thing was that I had no idea of how I would escape from them and also I assumed that I wasn't at the right place to look for the metal. But that wasn't so important at that moment. I thought of starting a conversation with them to see what they were up to.

"I am not here to disturb you", I said humming and hawing. "I've lost my way and got in there without wanting to."

The hairy creature turned back and started communicating silently, making gestures with the hairless hobs. After they had said a lot, they addressed me, "so, go back."

"You know", I said pitifully, "I can't because I'm closed inside because someone has blocked the entrance with rocks."

"Who?" He asked.

I replied, "Varvalakkas."

He then asked, "is he alive again?" He asked me in fear opening its eyes widely.

I said, "yes, he chased me and now I am closed inside."

It seems that, that piece of news was of vital importance because he immediately told the bad news to the hobs which seemed worried. Actually, some of them started moving back and disappeared in the tunnels. The hairy creature left after a while too and it was so scared and in a hurry that it threw the torch down and disappeared.

With a feeling of relief after this development, I proceeded and jumped into the river that was flowing before me and took the torch. I had just walked a few steps and I almost bumped into someone that was waiting for me. I made a few steps back and looked at the stranger who was staring at me with folded arms. His look was so piercing that I didn't bear to look at him for long. This look reminded me of my experience with Nohra in the cave and the warrior who got out of the ground. Maybe it's him, I thought. The only difference was in the tunic that he was wearing which was blue this time with little white stars. And on his head he had a wreath made of white metal which consisted of small joined lightning in two rows and in its center it had a weird shape.

"What did you think", I heard him saying, "that it would be easy? You'll see the last images of your life in here. Keep them. You won't see others because you will never be able to leave from here."

There was silence for a while and an unbearable feeling of embarrassment from my side and I was praying for something to happen but what was it? The back entrance was blocked by Varvalakkas and at the front the demon was waiting for my next move which was trying to go over him. I had no other choice. But how could I do this?

"If you", said the demon interrupting my thoughts, "have decided to die fighting for something impossible, why should you take this maiden with you who is completely innocent?" He found my weakest point there.

He was right. I would do what I had to at all costs. Why did she have to undergo the consequences of my actions? I know that it was a game he was playing. He was playing with my feelings to avert me from trying. But what if this wasn't true? How would Asteria go then? But even if that was true, she had more chances to survive if I went over him and moved on.

I had already made my decision and the demon predicted my next move and to make it clear to me that he wasn't joking, a roar was heard and in the demon's place there was a lion now showing me its teeth. I made one step hesitantly and the lion opened its mouth and made such a loud roar that it echoed to the underground cave and made my blood freeze.

I turned and looked at Asteria who nodded to me to go back. But if I went back, where would I go?

After all, that was exactly the demon's aim. Fear. Terrify me and make me return.

That filled me with determination and I made another step forward. Then the lion made another roar and was turned into an enormous snake with its head raised, hissing with its tongue going in and out, ready to attack its next prey.

It was just above my face and its horrifying eyes were magnetizing me; blocking every intention I had of resisting, while the flakes on its body were shiny moving all over. No, I said to myself. Don't be afraid. These are just images.

I closed my eyes so that I wouldn't look and made another step forward ready to accept the consequences of my decision. When I opened them I saw the demon again in its first form and his eyes threw flames.

"Do you dare to defy my power", he said loudly. Then he raised his hands and then in a V shape he lowered and joined them as if he was joining invisible threads. On his last move he kept them even more joined without stopping saying something in an unknown language. Then he stepped back and waited.

I was determined to continue what I was doing. I made a step forward and crashed on something hard. I touched it. It was frozen and hard. I made another step beside and tried to go over it but in vain. It was as if I was hitting onto a pane of glass. I ran left and right, I tried from a higher part, from a lower part. Nothing, there was an invisible impenetrable wall in front me.

A laughter that gave me the creeps was heard behind the invisible pane and the demon disappeared. I looked at Asteria. What should I do? What would we do? She was captive with me, too. She was going through what I was because of me, without a reason.

She was sitting scared inside the cave. As I was looking at her, I noticed a change on the appearance of her face which I thought reflected what was happening inside her. She wasn't that distant, indifferent, secret, cold mask I had first met. She now had a serious appearance which didn't repel you because I understood that she was taking active part, even if only with her feelings and changes in her psychology, in what was going on.

But I shouldn't call it a 'mask' because when you have a handicap which you are trying to hide because you don't want the others to feel sorry for you, you develop an aggressive behavior in order to protect yourself and you become introverted. The mask is something fake, superficial and connected with the character of the person wearing it.

I think that this analysis of my point of view satisfied only me. Because many times our knowledge on psychology becomes useless before the real facts. One thing was sure and I could see it clear. I looked at Asteria in a different way. I didn't feel pity or sorry for her problem. She was becoming more familiar to me and maybe more necessary. I saw that we would go through a lot together - if we managed to overcome this present, no escape situation - and that gave me a hidden relief which I couldn't explain.

What I had to avoid, though, was show her that I feel pity or sorry for her. That was the most difficult thing because everything I did included that risk regardless of the fact that I had no such intention. I stopped making these thoughts and returned to reality where the seeking of a solution was really urgent. We were buried in the depths of the Earth with no escape.

The humming of the underground river woke me up. I went back and looked at the place where it could be seen. There was enough space for someone to breathe and move at the underground river bed. That was the only solution. I couldn't think of another one. But I would have to explain to Asteria that I would make the attempt on my own and if I managed something, I would return to take her with me.

I explained it to her the best way I could. She nodded her head but she couldn't otherwise. I asked her if she was afraid and she made me understand that she would be praying. I left her the torch and prayed to God to help me.

I went down to the river carefully because the water was reaching my waist and made me freeze. I was holding the walls of the tunnel from one side but it was too difficult for me to walk. There were times when it reached my neck and others that it looked like a small waterfall because the ground was going down. So far I could breathe even though I had some difficulties. The only thing that was worrying me was if the river bed would become more narrow making it impossible for me to breathe.

And suddenly I discerned light. When I got closer to that point, the underground tunnel had another gap as in the beginning that I set off. The light was coming from a small hole on the ceiling of the cave and basically there was an exit there. Apart from the fact that it was really high up, the gap was too narrow.

I got out of the river which had made me freeze and gave a more careful look at the place. That cave was big and seemed to be extending further. I decided to follow it and if it led to a dead end, I would follow the river again. The main aim of finding the metal was really distant. I hadn't forgotten about it but our survival was above all. If we managed to survive, I would try again.

I followed the cave's direction and though I was far away and couldn't hear the river, it was in front of me again. A few meters away there was a natural well and its opening could fit one person. The river which could be seen on its bottom was creating a swirl.

The weirdest and most noticeable thing was that in the middle of the well there was a thick piece of wood; from a tree trunk maybe. There must have been something interesting in there. I bowed in great curiosity and looked at the inside. I noticed that something white could be discerned on its bottom. I looked again more closely and saw something like balls made of stone. The depth of the well must have been about three meters.

Have I come across the metal by accident? Going down to the well's bottom would be a good answer. The problem I would face was the swirl of the water that wouldn't let me be stable, it would drift me. I would hold on to the walls with my hands and feet. But how would I go down if my one hand was holding something? If I had a rope maybe…..

I looked around to find something that could help me but in vain. I stopped to think and I saw the belt I had around my waist. This is the solution, I said. I will tie its one end around the tree trunk and the other around my leg close to my ankle so that the swirl won't drift me.

I started going down carefully and I barely touched the stone balls, because the swirl was turning me and I had to use my feet as a 'brake'. I touched one with great difficulty and inspected it. It could fit in my palm but I didn't notice anything special on it unless the fact that it had a groove in its middle like an equator.

I tried to open it but it wouldn't. I climbed up with difficulty and put it down. How many were there at the bottom of the well? I went down again in order to count them by touch. I wasn't sure if there were eight or nine. The swirl didn't allow me to.

I did this route seven times and on the eighth my belt broke and got carried away by the river's current. I hit my back and my knee twice but then managed to stand. It was impossible to go back because the current of the river was violent. I couldn't do else but continue my course to find an end but I was suspecting that the river ended in a sea. I had to find an exit. How long could Astria wait for me? The balls would remain here if, of course, they were the silver ones.

I decided to move on. I picked up my belt and discovered that it wasn't broken. It just had been untied from the tree trunk. The river was becoming more violent and at some point I couldn't control my movements. It was drifting me. I was just trying to avoid the walls wherever that was possible. There was light in front of me and I realized that the river ended in a sea like I had predicted. Fortunately it was a full moon, I thought.

It really threw me into the sea and holding my breath I swam to its surface - about five meters. I was on the right side of Nanou's port. I breathed fresh air voraciously and tried to organize my thoughts. It was impossible to go back. So then what?

Would Asteria stay there for ever? I wouldn't bear that. The stones the Varvalakkas had thrown blocking the exit were difficult to be removed by only one person. Unless …

I went ashore and with the moonlight as a guide I climbed up the gorge again with a plan on my mind but I wasn't sure if it would succeed. I arrived at the place where the opening was closed by the rocks but didn't go till there. I climbed up to the top where I had seen Varvalakkas being formed and attempted something really daring, which was dictated to me by agony for Asteria's fate. I wasn't thinking about the silver metal. I had to save Asteria.

"Mithra", I shouted on top of my lungs, "Varvalakka. Apollo is my God and is stronger than you." I had just finished my sentence when I heard that terrible voice again and Varvalakkas was being formed below me in the gorge. That was my aim. If he wanted to throw rocks at me, he would have to use the same he used the first time.

Fortunately, I had predicted correctly and he started hurling the rocks at me. I averted two or three and then changed position because being on the sides I was trying to send him away in order to go down to the opening that led to Asteria. When I managed that, I discovered that there was a gap between the rocks from which I could pass and find the opening of the underground tunnel.

Varvalakkas realized what I was trying to do and started hurling rocks at the opening this time, blocking the entrance like he did the first time. But I wasn't afraid now. I had another solution. In agony I moved on and reached the place where the humming of the underground river was louder. I was expecting to see the light from the torch but there was nothing. The pang of anguish was became even stronger.

"Asteria", I shouted in a voice that sounded like a cry because of my agony for her. I was about to shout again when something touched my hand.

"Asteria", I said in a lower voice, "is that you?" I was so stupid. How could she answer me? She couldn't talk. I reached out my hands and tried to recognize her by touch. Yes, it was her. Thank God! I really wanted to hug her on impulse and tried hard not to do so.

"There are so many things that I want to tell you", I told her, "but I will tell you briefly what I have done to come here again, so I told her about my adventure in a few words. We just have to hold hands so that we won't get lost in the dark", I suggested.

We moved on and started carefully the route I had already traveled until we reached the well. There we had the moonlight which was coming in from the opening of the roof. I examined the stone balls again but couldn't find a solution. There were two more left at the bottom of the well and tried to bring them up in the same way.

I really managed to do so and brought the remaining two up. Nothing. I couldn't make heads or tails of it. They probably had nothing to do with the metal. Asteria then, picked one, took it in her hand to examine it but it slipped and fell onto the ground splitting in two. In the beginning I thought it had been broken but no. It opened in two parts and there was a gap inside it which was filled by a silver nugget.

"We've found it", I shouted with joy! We've found it by accident. But it doesn't matter, the result counts, I thought.

We had to organize our return now. I explained Asteria the route and the way we would go down the river. I would go down first. I would hold the end of the belt so that I wouldn't be drifted by the swirl and Asteria would go next. I went down and then helped her do the same.

I could take the belt but I was too tired and I left it in the well as a token. I told her to be careful in the river and when we were ready I left the belt and we drifted by the current. I was holding her hand tight and of course we had some small accidents like hitting on the walls just to remind us that the test wouldn't be so easy.

We arrived at the tunnel's exit, to the sea but there were some strange lights. I held on the walls and told Asteria to do the same. They were green and looked like luminous lights. I went near and discovered that they were weird fish which had something like a luminous antenna on their head. They were about seven, four inches big and seemed to be patrolling the area deterring us to exit.

They looked like those fish who live in great depths where there is no light. What was the use of the luminous antennas? Suddenly, Asteria tried to put her other foot on the rock and left my hand which caused her to slip and fall into the sea. Then a fish ran, touched her with its antenna and she stayed still like she was dead and began to sink. Without thinking I dived and pulled her up.

"What happened to you", I asked her worried, "are you OK?" She closed her eyes and opened them again after a while. I didn't know how to help her. After a few minutes she moved her fingers, then her feet and she almost came round. In the meantime the fish that had touched her became purple and left.

What did she feel with the touch of its antenna which paralyzed her? There was only one way to know. To undergo the same test. But if this should be done with all the fish which were guarding the exit, it would be better to do it in a way that we could save each other in turns until we eliminate the dangerous fish. The good thing was that only one fish left the group each time to attack us.

I explained my thought to Asteria so that she would be ready to pull me when the fish hit me. I fell into the water going to the exit and a fish left the group and touched me. I felt as if I had been struck by lightning, as if I was suffering electrocution and got paralyzed. I was too weak to move my finger. I felt Asteria pulling me out and in a few minutes the effect of the fish's antenna was over.

What I asked of Asteria when I came round was to let me go again this third time and then in turns. She accepted but with a lot of protesting, but that was what had to be done. She didn't have to suffer more times because of my test. Judging from her reaction I added another positive feature in her character.

When we were done with the fish we dove in; holding our breath and got out to the surface. The moon was tracing its route going down to hide behind the mountains. It seemed to me like it was the most beautiful full moon I had ever seen. My heart was fluttering and I didn't know why.

Maybe it was the joy for the positive outcome of our test or because we managed to survive through all the obstacles we had come across. Probably the latter. I couldn't even feel the exhaustion in my arms and legs. It was covered by the great satisfaction that we were alive after all the insurmountable difficulties we had went through.

I could hear birds singing and I felt as if it was day and not night after all. The way back was a pleasant route despite the hardships. It was almost dawn…

We arrived at the Temple of Evdomagetis Apollo, when the sun had risen from the East. I was shining with joy. Everyone noticed that, even Mystic Yetion. I gave the pot of the Rock Crystal with the silver nugget inside to the Mystic.

"We have got the second element", said Yetion. "You are worthy to be called 'Fighter of the Sun'".

My smile became even wider and felt as if I was higher that everyone. I really wanted to say that I wouldn't have made it if it hadn't been for Asteria's advice. But I shouldn't bring her here even with my thoughts. Aetion was waiting outside of the Temple to return to Okria. He wanted to know details about my second test. Despite my exhaustion I couldn't help telling him about our adventure but very carefully because I didn't want to show him that Asteria had played a great part in it.

I was back in my bedroom. Before going to sleep I couldn't help bringing back to my memory the scenes and moments of my test but also my life in Athens and Symi too. I wanted so much to return. This desire gave me the strength to fight with the demons every time and overcome all obstacles. I felt a sweet exhaustion all over my body which barely allowed me to bring back a few things from my childhood. My eyes didn't obey. I lay down and surrendered to the sweet mist of sleep.

Chapter 17

FREE FALLING

I had all the time I needed to rest, since I was allowed three days of resting before setting off for the third test, so I woke up without stress or agony nearly in the afternoon. Though the sun was shining, there was some kind of depression inside me due to my longing to return to the real world.

It's a terrible feeling to be in your native place and feel alone and isolated without being able to act normal and do whatever you want. I felt like a fish caught in the net which was trying to get free only to get more tangled up. My future was unknown and though my tests had a good end so far the joy for their outcome lasted only a while.

There was a long road ahead of me and it wasn't up to me to surpass the obstacles and hardships. Everything was so unpredictable, uncontrolled, without logic beyond human limits. There were times when I was trying to convince myself that it was just a long dream but after every awakening in the world of the spirits I confirmed my great misfortune and inability to escape and that drove me mad. I blamed everything and I often asked myself - why me? Why did this happen to me?

I was getting no logical reply. I had to go through all the tests. I had to undergo what I had been through and much more in order to be able to get myself out of this maze of virtual reality which was beyond my imagination.

The days went by quickly and the day for the third test arrived. Where would I go? In which place would I put into trial my physical and psychological powers and weaknesses? Aetion, punctual on his appointment, arrived knocking the door. I opened it and looked at him indifferently and maybe in a bad mood.

"Is there a problem", he asked me, guessing what was happening inside me because of my appearance and look.

"No", I replied unwillingly.

"So, are you ready", he asked.

"Yes", I said, "off we go."

I had just got out but went back to the room to take the blue sphere with me. Maybe it would be useful. I stood for a while to think. It was more of a burden and trouble actually so I left without it again. We arrived at the familiar Temple of Agitoras Apollo where Asteria was waiting and after taking her with us we set off east.

We got out of Okria and went down to a valley which could be seen from far away hidden behind the steep mountains. On its northern part was this Temple of Apollo, protected behind huge rocks. It was dedicated to Nouminios Apollo, according to what was written at the entrance of the outside door, and was very simple but firm and powerful, built on big carved rocks. It had very small windows that looked like embrasures and one unique entrance made of thick pieces of wood with iron casing for protection.

Silence was omnipresent as if there was nobody there. However, the door outside opened without anyone having seen us-as I thought- as well as the Temple's door and so we got in. A priest was waiting for us behind the door and guided us to the main temple through another door, announcing the Mystic.

"Mystic Ixion", he said, and I moved on with Asteria because Aetion had stayed outside. Ixion was sitting at a low seat reading a papyrus and didn't raise his head even though we got in. After a long time he finally stood up and looked at us thoroughly.

"Are you ready", He asked me.

"Yes", I replied in a low voice.

Ixion said, "the oracle for the test is the following: 'On top of Dysalotos, eighty meters below the circle of the old sun and three hundred and twenty meters above the ground, in the eagles' nest, is the metal'".

There was silence for a while and then Ixion addressed to me and said, "you've got will and courage, two necessary features for every fighter, which, if combined with calm thinking and patience, bring the right result."

Then he called Asteria and whispered something to her ear. She nodded her head and returned to her first place. When Mystic's voice was heard again, it was for us to take the pot which was at the statue's feet. It was similar to the previous we had taken but that one was made of Lapis Lazuli, the blue mineral.

Asteria took it and Ixion showed us the door. As we were getting out, the priest who was at the outside door was holding a large rope which he gave to me saying, "you will need it."

I put it over my head and and one arm and let it hang from my shoulder. It was thin and quite strong and I estimated it was eighty meters long, the same length as the distance to get to where the metal was, according to the oracle. I thanked him and we left the small valley and the Temple of Nouminios Apollo to return to Okria.

On to Dysalotos then. I was going to a place the mere landscape of which reminded you of how small, how insignificant you are. And though I thought that so far, no human foot had ever stepped on that vertical rock where I had to go, it seems that some others had already made it before me placing the zinc metal.

I had so many queries. The rope in order to reach the metal was eighty meters long. Why did the oracle say that it was three hundred and twenty meters more to the ground? I'm not that stupid to go down since it's so much easier to climb up again after I had got the metal. Even if I wanted to go down, the rope wouldn't be enough. Then what?

I stopped making those thoughts because I couldn't make head or tail of the whole situation and made one which really frightened me. Height... I couldn't bear being at high places because it made me nervous. We would see how I would fight that, which could end up being much worse that the demons that wanted to stop me.

I remember when my father brought me to Dysalotos as a young boy. He took me to the root of the vertical rock and told me: 'Look up'. When I did that, I felt dizzy. I thought that the mountain was about to fall on me. I was about to faint and left running, looking back all the time, while my father was laughing. Meanwhile, we reached Okria when Aetion said that we would move on, just the two of us, because Asteria would go somewhere else to watch my descent to the rock.

So we parted ways. Asteria went towards Amaxitis while Aetion and I headed north. We followed a narrow path which led us to a cypress forest which was getting thicker as we were moving on. At some places there were glades for farming.

We reached a place where the path was divided in two. Aetion stopped there and said, "you will follow the path on the right and reach the place the oracle dictated. I will return because I have other matters to attend to. Good luck."

Turning his back, he left leaving me alone for the first time to complete my test. I was really sad because I would have to go through everything on my own. Asteria, even if she couldn't talk, was some kind of consolation for me. Her presence was a support for my morale. I would have to surmount all obstacles alone. I had no other choice. Since those were the commands, I had to obey them.

As I was walking, the cypresses were diminishing - a sign that we were reaching the top. And while I was still in a cluster of trees, in a small glade I could discern a small house like the ones the shepherds build with stones. There was a man sitting outside who welcomed me with a smile. He was holding a knife with which he was carving a snake on a piece of soft wood.

"Welcome my lad", he said. I greeted him back and then he asked, "can I help you?"

"With what", I asked.

He replied, "you are moving straight to the precipice. Are you lost? Unless that's your destination." I didn't reply to him and I looked at him ignoring the way he stated the last sentence. Whether it was a verification or a wish.

He had a miserable face and a feigned smile. As if he had put it on deliberately. Maybe, of course, I was wrong in the judgement of this man's character and he really wanted to help. But in what could he help since I had to attempt everything on my own? The appearance, however, doesn't always reflect the inner world of a person, I thought, because so far I had been mistaken many times on that.

"I have something to do", I said after a long silence.

"That's why I'm telling you that", he answered. "I can help you."

I weighed it all on my mind but didn't decide to speak. How should I know what part he was playing?

"Aren't you going to the precipice", He asked persistently. I didn't answer and hurried to leave greeting him to avoid the pressure of his questions.

I was quite far when I heard him saying, "do you know how to fly"? I turned and looked at him in wonder because of that question. What did he mean if I know how to fly…

"You will need it", he added.

This sentence required much discussion about the irony it was hiding. But I wouldn't waste my time with someone who wanted to know where I was going only out of curiosity. Lonely people like him can't help starting a conversation and asking millions of things when they see someone; only to get out of their boredom and loneliness. So there was no reason to answer only to begin a conversation. I smiled unwillingly and carried on my course.

I arrived at another deserted shepherd's house and could see that I was reaching the top of the vertical rock as everything had moved aside to let the magnificence of the stone giant appear. As I was getting out of the cypress cluster I could see the end of the road and the beginning of my trials.

The crest of the steep rock was waiting for me; painted by the bright sunlight as if it was made of gold. Some small summer birds were jumping non-stop on the big lonely cypress which was a few meters far from the precipice breaking the silence and tranquility that were omnipresent.

The view from the top was unique. Far way at the East, at the Minor Asia coast, silver mirrors in the sea were reflecting the sun rays moving rhythmically while at the nearby mountains the cypresses had settled at every crevice of the rock. How did they manage that? It was a wonder of the nature but also of the strength and the willingness to live.

I moved towards the cypress wondering at which point of the precipice I should attempt my descent. I was close to the trunk and to my surprise I saw that near it on a rock which was towards the East, there was a carved circle like the one the Head Priestess Psamanthi had shown us at the Temple of Agitoras Apollo.

It must have been carved many centuries ago because the rain and sun had made its surface smooth. What did that circle mean up here on the crest of the precipice? I brought back to my mind the oracle and stopped at the phrase 'under the circle of the old sun'.

That's it, I thought. The carved circle was depicting the sun that used to be worshiped many years ago and was looking at the first sun rays as soon as it rose from the East. So logically, the metal was eighty meters under that steep rock.

I made a few steps in front of the tree and immediately went back and held on its trunk. Everything was turning around me and my legs couldn't hold my body. I felt my stomach about to go out from my mouth and I was drenched in a cold sweat.

I waited a few minutes to pass, then crawled toward the edge of the rock and looked again. I closed my eyes so that I wouldn't look. The same mood again. I went back and sat at the root of the tree to calm down.

I could hear the waves on the pebbles of the beach and this sound was coming to my ears like a whisper from an undefined conversation whose words I couldn't understand. As much as I tried to listen, it didn't make sense. I wasn't sure whether it was just noise from the waves.

I isolated that noise and tried to understand it really hard. For a moment, I discerned something. Something louder. One word. Only one word dominated. It was heard silently but steadily inviting me to attempt it.

"Fly", it was saying, "Fly."

It was dictating it to me in a commanding, persistent way. As if there wasn't a landscape around me, all my senses had disappeared only my hearing remained to perceive this signal.

I surrendered to the command of that voice and stood up mechanically without realizing it and moved forward. I was feeling a pull, a force pulling me down which paralyzed my all my limbs. I wanted to fly. I wanted to let myself fly on empty space. I didn't care about the end. Those moments when I would be floating, would be as if I were in a sweet fog, a dream place where I could rest myself. Something stronger than me was telling me to do it.

I left the rope of my hand and went to the edge of the precipice. I closed my eyes and lifted one leg keeping my balance with the other before my flying. Suddenly, to the images in my mind came Asteria's face. Melancholic, sad with an expression of wondering on her lips and eyes. I was agitated.

I opened my eyes and saw what I was about to attempt, in fright. I made a step backwards and fell on my back and my heart was beating so fast that it felt like it was about to break. I remained in this position until I calmed down and gain my self-control. No, I said loudly, and punched the ground. I won't give Nohra the pleasure to see me failing.

My feet felt as if I had been walking all day. I couldn't move them. They didn't obey me. But my hands didn't feel better either. Much time passed until I managed to pull myself together and organize my thoughts. I had to try it. It was inevitable. But I needed to organize the best way I could and think calmly.

The safest solution was to tie the one edge of the rope around the tree trunk and the other around my chest so that even if it slipped from my hands, I would be able to hold on in another way. I checked the knot I had tied around the cypress and tied myself carefully. In order to test if it was OK, I weighed my body on a branch and saw that it worked.

I seemed to be ready physically, but not psychologically. I still didn't dare to think that beneath my feet there were four hundred meters of empty space. Just the thought of it made my limbs tremble. I was feeling weak as if I had just recovered from a serious illness. Still, I had to do it.

I set off again for the edge of the precipice, trying not to think of the height. I must be looking like someone who was about to be executed. Suddenly, something big passed overhead. I looked up and saw a huge eagle flying over me. It was enormous. So enormous that it could lift me with its claws. It flew over me two or three times more and left east.

"Thank God", I said. Now that he has left its time for me to descend.

I reached the edge of the precipice and turned backwards so that I won't look. It was better that way. I just couldn't decide to put my foot on the space. I held on to the rope and made the first step.

I have to, I told myself; clenching my teeth so hard that my jaws hurt. I changed hand and foot and was on the empty space of four hundred meters depth, a mouth ready to swallow you, which asks for atonement only with the corpse of the unholy who will dare to step on it.

The weight of the body multiplies and goes to the hands to keep it from falling to the ground. I climbed down a little bit more and stopped to rest. For this reason I stepped on the rope with one foot and tied the other. I didn't dare to look down. After a while I climbed down quite a few meters but my shoulders were hurting me. I estimated I had done half the way when I heard a weird scream and then hoots. Suddenly, enormous eagles and other predatory birds who had got out of their nests, appeared .

Eagles with black wings, gray eagles and hawks, were instigated with screams as if someone had warned them about something important that was about to happen. That important thing was my descending near their nests. I had disturbed their quietness, actually I saw that there were eggs in their nests when I went near. So they wanted to send away the intruder for fear of me harming their eggs. Of course someone had agitated them because their attitude towards me wasn't at all friendly.

I rushed to descend more quickly without paying attention to my hands which were burning by the rubbing of the rope, nor was I paying attention to my shoulders which felt as if they had nails driven in them. I had to descend much quicker to reduce the consequences of the rock's tenants which were flying near me touching me in order to scare me and make me let go off the rope.

I must have been a few meters far from my final destination and for a moment the sky got dark and I saw the enormous eagle that I had met before my descending. It was flying above me terrifying me with the way it was hooting and its sharp claws were projected.

I was at the end of the rope when the eagle attacked me. It didn't hit me with its beak but with its head in an attempt to get me off the rope. The result was my becoming a pendulum and my hands were bleeding on the rocks and my fingers were wounded and hurting me. When I managed to steady myself, the eagle got ready for another attack and I wasn't sure if it would use its beak that time.

I tried to go to the end of the rope as fast as I could, and before I made it I saw a cave with stalactites and stalagmites before me. Its size was like a small room but what I noticed and didn't like was that it seemed to be the enormous eagle's nest which was trying to knock down - the uninvited visitor. Now I realized why it was so hostile towards me.

I stepped on the ground of the cave the moment that the eagle was getting in like a bullet. I moved beside to avert it and hid behind a stalagmite which was joined with a stalactite creating a column two inches thick. The eagle got in forcefully and stopped in front of its nest; looking at the eggs inside in order to check whether there was one missing.

The nest was made of osier branches and hay which were spread inside the nest. Inside were seven very large eggs. What impressed me the most was that one of the eggs wasn't the same color as the rest. I suspected that it was the one which had the metal inside because its size wasn't the same as the rest either. It seemed that it had been placed there the same days the eagle had laid its eggs because it regarded the egg as its own.

The eagle checked the eggs with its beak and then sat on them carefully; relieved that they were OK. It was very impressive with black and brown wings, yellow claws and beak. Its neck was decorated with white feathers which looked like a necklace. What do I do now, I thought. How will I make the eagle go away and take the egg inside which may be the zinc?

The floor consisted of its victims' bones which was a macabre thing to see. Wherever you stepped you could hear the sound the bones make when they crash each other. Goats, lamps and other smaller animals may have been prey to the claws of that merciless predator.

When the eagle sat on its eggs, reassured that they were OK, it was relieved. At times, though, it turned toward me and looked bitterly. A frozen look which showed the decisiveness and power of the king of the fowls. To scare me more, it also hit its wings to show me that it was ready to attack any time. If it hadn't been for the eggs, it would have chased me everywhere to kill me. But it was taking care of protecting them and maintaining the appropriate temperature.

So, thanks to the eggs I was enjoying this peculiar immunity. Unfortunately for me I had to find a way to get the egg which could be achieved only if the eagle went away. How would that be done? No one knew. I had nothing in mind. I was just waiting to see if something would happen.

While I was looking around the cave, behind me there were bones of a big goat. More specifically from its scalp and some pieces of its limbs. Near them there were stones on which it seemed that water from the cave's roof was dripping. The rocks had become white and smooth; maybe because of the chalky sediments that the water contains.

I thought about it when I saw them again and I chose one whose size matched the eggs. I don't know how I would do it, but it was the only solution. To change the egg, which I hoped had the metal in, with that stone. The upper surface was fine. I couldn't say the same for the lower surface, though.

I carefully made one step to go near but the noise produced when stepping on the bones made the eagle turn towards me to open its mouth and wings to show me that it was alert. Thankfully it didn't leave the eggs. I took the stone and saw that luckily it was symmetrical but it had a different color underneath.

I was holding it in my hands examining it when a loud noise was heard from outside and stones were thrown from above in great force. Some of them passed in front of the cave's entrance and some small ones hit on the floor's edge.

The eagle sat on its nest. Its wings were raised which was a sign of its irritation and it looked outside worried. A voice like the previous was heard which made the fowls restless again and more stones fell down making too much noise. A big stone hit on the cave's ground broke into pieces and scattered all over the place.

Fortunately, I was behind the stalagmite's column. A piece hit on it causing the eagle to scream while some smaller pieces hit it and made him stand up. The eagle got out and went to a spot where he could look up and then the following amazing things happened. First a voice from above was heard which reminded me of my previous encounter.

"I asked you if you could fly because you would definitely need it now", he said laughing and I recognized that it was the hermit. The next minute the edge of the rope where I had tied around the cypress trunk got untied without a reason. As it was falling down it hit the eagle on the face and made it get dizzy and trip.

I didn't think about it. I immediately ran and took the egg with my hands shaking and put the stone in its place as fast as I could, while the hermit's creepy laughter echoed all over the place. The rope was hanging down and the eagle was coming round shaking its head as if it wanted to take something off.

When I returned to the place where I was sitting I realized how tragic my position was. The hermit, as I suspected, was obviously one of Nohra's demons. He untied the rope and I was left alone with the eagle without being able to climb up.

There was an empty space of three hundred and twenty meters beneath me and all I had was an eighty-meter rope. I felt desperate. I thought about the hermit's words 'if I know how to fly'. Indeed. only if I could fly, would I be able to save myself. I couldn't think logically and I had no idea how I would escape from this prison.

In the meantime, the eagle had recovered its senses completely and went inside the cave near the nest. It stood over the eggs checking them. When I had taken the egg I immediately hid it in my leather backpack I always had with me for fear of the eagle seeing it.

The eagle moved the stone I had put in the place of the egg I had taken. He was relieved mainly because of its weight rather than its shape as I had camouflaged it among the other eggs. Sure of the number of the eggs it got in and sat on them. At least I didn't have to worry about that anymore.

The time was passing by and I was looking at the bones on the cave's floor making depressing thoughts about my future. Without having anything else to do, I started picking up the rope which was hanging out of the cave. The noise it produced as it was crawling among the bones had made the eagle restless and worried. When I picked it up I thought of something. Tie it around the stalagmite's column and start descending so as to see if I could make a few stops. But if I found a place to stop, how would I untie its edge from the stalagmite?

Something flashed on my mind and saw the problem from another perspective. Instead of tying the edge around the stalagmite, it would be better if I turned it around it many times and then tie its edge around me. In that way, I would have both the edges tied on me and I would descend with a double rope. When I found a place to stop, I would do the same trick maybe around a bush.

The only thing was that the rope would be forty meters instead of eighty. The only thing that wasn't sure was that I would find a place to stop in a distance of forty meters. But whichever distance would be ok. I couldn't think of another solution so I decided to make an attempt.

I put the rope around the stalagmite and tied myself. Being very careful and trying to be quiet I moved towards the exit. The eagle saw me and made a move but didn't leave the eggs. I reached the edge and holding on to the double rope I started abseiling.

After the first descent I didn't pay much attention to the fear and the giddiness. Besides, I had got over the first shock and my survival was more important than my mission. My shoulders as well as my palms were hurting me but I had no time to think of such things.

Half the way, I saw a bush which always grows in inaccessible places and its got white flowers. In Symi we call it Attoulas. It was big and I think it could bear my weight until I tied the rope around its trunk. The only bad thing was that it wasn't directly in front of me so I had to move right about three to four meters. When it was straight at me I pushed the vertical rock with my foot and started swaying, accelerating more and more until I reached and held on one branch. I stabilized myself with one hand and I was nearly at the end of the rope. But that was fine. It was a good thing that I had found that bush. Forty or thirty five meters didn't make a difference.

What if I didn't find another place to tie the rope as I was moving on? As soon as I thought of that I had cold sweat. I would stay hanging there like a scarecrow as a loot for the stone giant for disobeying it and become prey for the vultures of the place.

While I was about to tie the rope around Attoulas to stabilize myself and then untie one edge to to take it of the stalagmite, I hesitated and postponed it. I bent to see if there were other parts from which I could hold on. I noticed there was one bush and another one near it. I would really like to find another one. Anyway, I shouldn't torture my mind because I felt my shoulders burning due to the pain.

I held the trunk with one hand and with the other I untied the edge around my waist. Immediately the whole rope slipped and fell down. That moment I was holding only from one hand. I quickly grasped with my other hand the rope which was ties around me and reeled it around the trunk. To be able to stabilize myself and free myself, I let go of the rope and tied my waist again. Then I left only one row of the rope on the trunk and shared it evenly so that I could descend again keeping it double.

After much time I managed to have five stops. Two at an Atoullas, two at holm-oaks and one at a stick which was deep inside a rock which had probably been placed there by someone else before me. I estimated that three more stops remained and I would finish because I couldn't bear the pain in my hands. One stop was at another stick.

Unfortunately, after that there was nothing more to stabilize the rope before the ground. There were two stops left, that is another eighty meters. Then I thought that the rope was only eighty meters. So what? So, I would reach the ground with a single rope. That's what I did.

I was more than half way there when I stepped on a hole in order to rest. To my bad luck what I stepped on was a bee hive of wild bees who got out and started biting me all over my body. So I gave a push to start swaying so as not to pass in front of them and hurried to descend as fast as I could. But they kept chasing me and biting me. I was about four meters above the ground so I untied the rope and let myself fall down from that height. I couldn't bear it anymore. Luckily I fell on some osiers and lost my senses.

I don't know how I long I had stayed there, but I felt someone touching and nudging me. I opened my eyes and saw Asteria. I smiled at her and closed them again. I didn't have the courage to stand up. My limbs were hurting me; from my shoulders and palms to the muscles and the rest of my body because of the bites and my falling down.

The rope was left hanging and when I opened my eyes I recognized the place where my dad had taken me and had told me to look up. I was scared anymore, neither did I want to leave for fear of the mountain falling on me. I had descended it overcoming my fears and weaknesses.

When I fully came around I asked Asteria how she had arrived there and she showed me a boat with oars. She made me understand that a ship had brought it from Nanou. We got inside and took the oars. The sun was about to set and I was returning from my third test successfully. I had found the zinc.

As soon as I thought of that I quickly took out the egg which was made of stone and examined it. I didn't even want to think what would happen if the metal wasn't there. I couldn't bear it. It had a notch in the middle and I got out to see if I had made the right choice. I hit it on a stone and to my great joy the zinc clot rolled near me and I was so relieved. Now I could go to Nanou feeling calm.

We arrived without any unexpected incidents and headed for Amaxitis, having pulled the boat out of course. I would go to the Temple of Nouminios Apollo with Asteria to give the metal but the sun had already set and it was getting dark. So we headed for the Temple of Asteria. I left her there and as I was about to leave when Head Priestess Psamanthi called me.

"You can stay here tonight", she said, "and in the morning you can go to the Temple of Nouminios Apollo with Asteria."

What she said gave me great relief because I was about to faint because I was so tired. I thanked her and accepted her offer delighted. She guided me to a small room where the travelers and visitors sought rest after their long walking. I opened the door and, as far as I remember, it had a bed and a window.

In the morning when I woke up I discovered that it had a table and two chairs. The sleep had helped me regain my strength and my good mood. I went out and came across Asteria, who was waiting patiently, sitting down. We set off right away.

When we arrived at the Temple of Nouminios Apollo, there was great noise and the Priests were coming and going. We finally heard that three snakes had got into the Temple and they were trying to take them out. They took us to Mystic Ixion, who was sitting calm on a pedestal. He smiled as soon as he saw us and took the metal from the hands of Asteria which was in the pot made of Lapis Lazuli and said, "you have won despite your fear and the giddiness. You can now be called 'warrior of will', because with the power of your will, you are the winner in this test."

Warrior of will, I repeated to myself and smiled full of self confidence and pride. It was a difficult test and what I tried more was my own stamina. We left and during our return my mind kept going back to my home and my neighborhood. I was closed to myself and Asteria to her own, not being able to talk. Two different, parallel worlds which met because of some space-time oddity.

Chapter 18

The trial at Dysalonas made me really tired. My shoulders and arms were still in pain because of my over trying with the ropes but the good end and the experiences I had gained alleviated and relieved the pains. I think that in three days I would rest and then be able to try again with no problems.

It was true that I had reached the utmost limit regarding my fear with this trial, but it also tested my endurance in difficult decisions that required patience and calmness. It was ever harder because Asteria, who gave me courage and supported me, wasn't with me. Of course, I received all these only from her presence as she had never told me that she wanted to help me. How could she though? She couldn't talk. She was always very prim, without exaggerations and within the limits as she had been advised to be by the Mystics who made her make a vow about this. So, I couldn't wait for something more that what she seemed to be able to offer.

I probably asked too much from a Priestess who was used to the strict stiffness of the Temple and only knew how to perform her hieratic duties since she was a child and her parents had offered her to Apollo.

What did I ask of Asteria? I didn't have a specific answer nor could I define it.

Chapter 19

On the second day, I got out to Okria to stretch my legs and change images. The sun started rising and I arrived at the open air school with small kids. The teacher was explaining the arrival of the sun's sons and God's activities. I heard him saying:

> "Apollo is leaving in a few months in autumn and he is going to the Hypernorth country. When he returns, everything shines and they all praise him. The animals of Apollo are the wolf, the deer, the roe, the swan, the hawk, the crow, the magpie, the rat, the grasshopper, the cicada and the vulture."

He was asking the kids about these animals and each one was naming one until the group of animals was completed. Then he asked who the sons of the sun are and they all answered, "the Dorieis."

"Who guided them", he asked.

"Apollo Agitor", replied all together.

I moved on and left the teacher talking about Apollo and his achievements and his symbols which are the bow, the arrow, the lyre and the palm tree. At the Varouha valley the ripened wheat were waving like gold waves moved by the wind and he mules were carrying things from Amaxitis.

I was approaching the end of the road when someone behind a half-opened door, waved me to go there. I didn't know him. I stopped. He waved to me again and then vanished.

I went very carefully and bent to see who he was and someone pulled me from the shoulders and I got in by force. The door shut and I was in a room with a very weird decoration. On the walls there were drawings of processions which proceeded holding various objects and strange symbols filled the gaps between the drawings.

Fire was burning in a round, metal opened pot on the floor at which they must have thrown various herbs making the atmosphere suffocating. When I inhaled them they caused me to get dizzy so I leaned against the wall and started looking at the drawings. There was a door across this room in which a dwarf was standing dressed in a red tunic and behind him people with sad faces dressed in rugs had thronged.

The dwarf moved forward to the center and that bizarre group of people followed him. They looked lost - limping and stumbling. Most of them were mutilated in the limbs. They didn't have fingers, arms or legs and others were disfigured in the face. They thronged behind the dwarf's shadow; breathing heavily as if they had walked long distances.

"Do you know who these people are behind me", asked the dwarf.

"No", I said curious.

Then the dwarf said:

> "They were presumptive heroes like you, ambitious, selfish and vain who went beyond the limits in order to be admired by the people around them. They wanted everyone to look up to them and be considered more gods rather than humans.
>
> It's the same vanity that motivates the deprived ones to find paradise. They set this as a goal of their life and want to outdo the others in deprivations and prayers in order to achieve eternity, as they think. But unfortunately for them, as soon as they pass away only a few relatives remember them. After their death remains the oblivion and the silence.

They think that they will be remembered eternally and will make such a big impression, similar to the gigantic waves which are caused by the falling of a huge rock into the sea, but the wave they finally bring about is like the one caused by a little boy throwing a stone. The small ripples by the falling of that small stone represent the years that they will be remembered and die out after a while. Is that what you want to become?"

I began to say, "I want to."

"Come on. I'll show you", he said and asked me to follow him. He looked at me in the eyes so I obeyed without thinking about it. "Follow me", he said.

He moved too fast for someone so short, while the human scarecrows were running behind him to catch him up. We were passing by doors of different rooms with bizarre decorations of monsters and we were nearly running. After quite some time, we climbed up a big staircase and at its end there was an underground entrance with luxurious steps and I could see bright light.

"Come down to find out the truth", he said. "The Chthonic are waiting for you. They have sent me to call you. Come down." And he started descending.

I heard a voice behind me as soon as I made the first step.

"Don't do it", the voice screamed. "For Apollo's sake, don't do it!"

I turned to see who was shouting. It was probably a shepherd, as I could tell from his clothes.

"Why are you doing this", he asked me and suddenly a crash was heard and then the whole scenery of the dwarf and the human rugs vanished. I turned in front of me and to my fright I realized that I was on the brink of a precipice about to fall. I made a step behind and sat on a stone.

"Why do you want to fall", the shepherd asked me again coming closer. "Has Chasocrates brought you?"

"Who is this", I asked.

"Don't you know Chasocrates, also known as Kalostrates", was the reply.

"No", I said.

Then he said, "he appears to lonely people, pretending he wants to help them and makes his victims follow him to precipices and asks them to fall."

"Has he got any relation with Nohra", I asked.

"He is one of Nohra's people", he said.

I stood up and set off my returning after thanking the shepherd. If it hadn't been for him, I would surely have broken my neck at the precipice. And as they say, if you are a spirit and you die for a second time, you disappear forever. I returned having had another bad experience. Nohra and his people were lurking everywhere and I had to be even more careful. I shouldn't trust anyone.

Chapter 20

THE PROPHET'S ORACLE

The day of my fourth trial dawned and Aetion came again for the usual route. We would go to the old Daphniei settlement where the Temple of Karnios Apollo was and in which Mystic Melas has settled its citizens had abandoned it. But before all we went to pick Asteria up from the Temple of Agitoras, as always.

The Temple of Karnios Apollo was a bit far from the Daphniei settlement and was on the side of the sea at the end of the plateau which was leading down to the small port. It had strong fortification with huge rocks and looked over Alopos Cape at Minor Asia and of Kamiros town on the island of Rhodes. It also looked over the small islands Teftlousa which were gathered near the island of Symi living in their own world.

The sun was very hot even though it wasn't very high yet. We got into the yard and saw Priestesses in the middle of a ceremony. We remained there watching when one of them came and guided to the

Temple. Mystic Melas was praying in front of the God's statue and we waited for him to finish.

Aetion stayed outside, Asteria and I were at the entrance. When the Mystic finished, he invited us in. he was wearing a gray tunic and a skullcap of the same color. Light wind was blowing through the window of the Temple making the atmosphere cooler.

"I have nothing to tell you", he said. "A boat is waiting for you at the port to take you to the location where the fourth test will take place. The oracle will be given by Prophet Evdemonas, who you'll meet on the island of the lepers. The returning from this island will be done in your own way. Before you leave, take the sacred pot from the God's feet."

Asteria took the pot which was exactly similar to the others, made of alabaster, and we left right away. Outside, Aetion had all the details we needed to reach the boat, which was at the port.

This test seemed very strange to me. The Mystic wouldn't give us the oracle and it must be told by some Prophet whom we will reach by boat but we will return by our own means. How? By swimming maybe? There were no specific, clear instructions and I was confused. Anyway, since that was the way things should be done, we should follow the procedure. Asteria and I boarded and Aetion waved us goodbye.

We set sail and the captain manoeuvred and got quickly out the port. The breeze was blowing on the sails and we were heading south towards the small islands. The distance wasn't so long but it was too long for someone to cover it swimming. Besides I didn't know the hidden dangers of such an attempt.

After quite some time and as the wind was blowing even stronger, we reached the small islands. We knotted at the biggest rock which seemed to be used for that cause because there was a hole around which they tied the ropes.

There were three islands. In the biggest one, a few cedars and lentisks were grown and in the middle one 'artikia', which is a kind of plant with a long and thick trunk which is soft inside like a cork and can be carved easily. That's why fishermen use it quite often as buoys because it doesn't absorb much water and it is very light.

The third and smallest island had skoullous, which is a kind of wild leek and with its long branches in the middle and its flower on top which looked like a ball. It gave the impression of being part of a dream decoration from fairytales.

Unfortunately, if things were different I would have the time to enjoy the nature and tranquility. But now I looked at everything superficially without emotions because of my agony and stress for the test. Each island was about fifty meters away from the other. What troubled me was where Prophet Evdemon was.

No sooner had I finished my thought than Asteria pointed at something. There was someone sitting on top of the mountain watching something. Since that was the only human presence there, I supposed it was the Prophet. We headed for the top and when we reached the foot of the mountain, we discerned a cave and I counted that there were twelve steps going down. The Prophet kept looking and from what I understood he was watching the martins that had their nests there. That's weird, I thought. Why is he interested in watching the birds flying?

I was also curious to find out how did a person spend his time alone on an island which you could walk around in almost two hours. It's hard to understand what a person is thinking, what he is hiding inside and how he perceives everything. But that person was more interesting than anyone because he was a Prophet. He could predict the future which was a gift from god Apollo. The cave we saw was probably his oracle or his residence.

As I was thinking about all these, he suddenly stood up and started coming down. We were waiting for him patiently because his age didn't allow him to jump the steep rocks as a young man could do.

When he came closer, we saw a middle-aged man with a long beard but without much hair. He had a leather bag on his shoulder and when he stopped in front of us what impressed the most was his eyes. His one eye was white, which meant that he was blind and the other had a penetrating look as if his whole energy and power went through it.

We greeted each other and he said, "you don't have to tell me anything. I know why you are here. I have been waiting for you for a long time. This meeting has been programmed a long time ago. Everything happens for a reason. The whole universe functions under a predetermined plan made by the great Mind." There was silence for a while and all you could hear was the wind blowing and the waves splashing on the rocks.

"Let's go to my shelter", he said smiling and set off heading for the underground cave we had seen previously. He was supported by a long cane and his clothes, which were strips weaved together, were made of goat's fur. They were also colorful and made him look rather weird. The colors on his tunic, which was tied around his waist, were basically four. Brown, white, black and various shades of gray.

We began climbing down the twelve steps of the cave and saw a narrow room on the right, while on the left there was a small space which looked as if it used to have a human-sized egg there, which was removed but its shape remained there. The main room was divided by a low wall which had an entrance in its center and was basically the border between two rooms. Its room had some kind of bed made of stones but only one of the two seemed to be used.

The other one didn't have sheets; only dry algae forming a thick layer. The bed which was used by the Prophet had a textile made of goat's fur unfolded on the layer of algae. The table and chairs were made of cedar, probably by him. There were only two seats and the table was so uneven that you couldn't find a place to put something on without it falling down.

The Prophet didn't need luxuries and comforts and besides, he didn't expect any visitors on that secluded island. There was also a kind of fireplace at one corner and on the ceiling there was an opening which functioned as a window for light and fresh air.

At the other corner, there was a wooden construction which looked like a loom and from that room's roof, wooden cages were hanging made of artikia in order to be light and inside them there was food to protect it from the rodents. They contained cheese and olives. There were also two earthenware jars; one with oil and the other with water or wine and other cooking utensils. On the walls there were tools and two pieces of goat leather.

In a few words, he had everything he needed to survive on the island.

The Prophet sat on that kind of bed and showed us the chairs. I kept looking in curiosity and interest at all these objects in the cave feeling admiration for the fact that he was able to survive on such meager sources. Suddenly he was heard saying, "I have to tell you that you must stay here tonight because the test will have to start tomorrow for a number of reasons."

As he was talking, the wind became stronger and there were clouds gathered in the sky above the island because the light was reducing or becoming brighter at times. "Come I'll show you my agricultural activities", he said smiling and we went up to the surface again.

Next to the cave he had constructed an underground 'sterna' in the shape of a pot which was used to save up the water from the rain. There were two thrown 'curves' nearby used for fishing as he told us made of osier branches which he dived in the sea with stones which he tied around their lower part in order to make them sink. He put algae and sea-urchins inside, which he broke in order to lure the fish and have more for food.

We went to the northern part of the island which was covered by the mountain. There were six big olive trees and three almond trees giving him their fruit. He had also planted wheat, barley and legumes and in the summertime he grew other garden produce which he used to water with salty water from the well.

"He didn't ask for more than he wished for", he said. He wanted to be alone, to meditate and relax. Because what he predicted made him miserable. The clouds got thicker and as were returning, it started raining. We sat inside and I couldn't wait to hear the oracle and also the reason he had chosen to live alone on that island.

As if he had been reading my thoughts, he began to say:

> "I will tell you the oracle tomorrow morning. As far as the reason why I've chosen to live here, it's a long story but I'll narrate it to you in a few words.
>
> I used to live in Knidos when one day a rich man from Loryma invited me to make a prediction for him because his crop didn't go so well. He had sent a boat to take me there but on the way there was a strong wind. The mast broke and the sails were torn. Everyone on the crew thought that I was responsible for the bad weather and decided to throw me into the sea to make it calm. So they threw me and I was left to fight with the waves. I was looking at these islands from far away and was trying to approach them but the currents took me far

away. I prayed to god Apollo to help me and suddenly the currents changed and threw me ashore.

On my attempt to hold onto the rocks, a big wave came and threw me out and I fainted. When I opened my one eye - because that day I became blind from the other - I saw some appalling faces staring at me. They didn't have ears, noses, lips and they had scars and wounds all over their body. When they saw that I got scared and stepped behind, they calmed me down saying that I wasn't in danger by them.

Appalling though they were, their hearts were filled with kindness. They took care of me with whatever they had to help me recover and gain back my powers. I spent six weeks in that bed. They were lepers, exiled to the island. They used to live outside the town. The reason why they had sent them away was this:

One day when there was a celebration for the Vaκhos for the beginning of the new wine crop and according to the tradition everyone was wearing masks, drinking and dancing, the lepers got jealous and wanted to drink and dance too. They knew that nobody would allow them to do so. Then one of them thought that it would be a good idea to wear masks too so that no one could recognize them. That's what they did. They put on masks and started drinking, dancing and singing. But when you drink much, you can't control yourself, so some of them got drunk and threw their masks and revealed their scars. They were immediately gathered and the following day they were exiled to this island.

I lived with them for seventeen years. We all used to live together in this cave. They had a small boat and in that they went to Nanou to be given from a distance, food and clothes by the people of Okria. But one day they didn't manage to return because of the bad weather which caused their boat to sink and they all drowned. Since then I have been living alone on this island because I loved it. It accepted me and provided me with safety when I was in danger. I got used to the life here and organized my stay the best I could.

The wind and rain got worse and the atmosphere in the cave had some kind of sweetness with the Prophet narrating us stories and us hanging upon his words.

"How are you able to predict the future", I asked him.

He smiled and said, "it's hard for me to explain, but all I can say is the means I use. Mainly from the way birds fly, that's why you saw me on that top watching the martins and also from the clouds, the ants and other omens."

As he was talking, I had an idea which I was afraid of saying. I finally got the courage and said, "have you foreseen what I will do? Will I remain a spirit or be able to escape?"

He sat back comfortably touching his beard and I was eagerly awaiting his reply.

He replied, "our desires and yearnings are birds that fly outside; many times having the size of our power and sensibility. Between the dream and reality they are a glow in time. You can't look at both sides at the same time. Everything changes so fast that our desire becomes aversion the next minute. You have to decide what you really want."

I remained looking at him, waiting that he would go on talking but nothing. What he had told me didn't make sense, except for the last phrase 'you have to decide what you really want'. What to decide. I knew what I wanted in my heart. To return. Nothing could stop me.

The wind was blowing really strong and the rain was whipping the small islands of the lepers which seemed to be about to sail away. A few rain drops began coming in from the roof and the steps at the entrance had got wet. The Prophet probably didn't want to reveal the end to me though he knew it really well. Well, that made sense because otherwise I wouldn't try at all.

"The future isn't always defined because the man gives his feelings to the objects which didn't have a soul. So, a part of what was meant to be in the first place, may change on the way with the man's participation. That's why I can't tell you with certainty what you will do", he said reading my thoughts again.

So I came back to the point where I thought I would learn something about the outcome of my tests and the final result. We saw a kind of grid outside the cave. It had an undefined shape of a trap-door. Mystic placed it at the opening and tied it from inside blocking the entrance in that way.

"I have put this for protection", he said, "for you mainly."

His pointing out seemed weird to me and didn't understand it. Later he asked me about the other trials I had gone through and he seemed to be enjoying listening to the ways I used to carry out my mission. The night was going by and the first signs of sleep came to my eyes. The Mystic realized it and gave us the signal first.

"Friends", he said, "it's time to rest our body and he lied down in his bed." So we went to our beds too. Asteria went to the one which was more inside.

The Prophet had placed a textile on it earlier. I made myself comfortable in the egg's shell.

My eyes were closing because of tiredness and the next minute they opened as if someone or something was nudging me. This kept on for some time when suddenly after everything was calm after the storm, and not a leaf was moving, a clatter was heard outside the cave.

As far as I remember, the only animals I had seen on the island were goats and horses. But the clatter that was heard was of a big animal. After some time, the clutter was heard again. In fact it was of two animals at the same time. Then, waves splashing were heard and the clutters were now of more animals. In the meantime, shouts and sounds of a battle were heard and the clutters became even louder as if there was a cavalry charge.

I got up and looked at the cave inside. Asteria had also woken up and was sitting at her bed. The Prophet was still sleeping while the screaming and shouting of the warriors were breaking the silence.

"In the cave, in the cave they are hiding. Let's go and get them", said one of those who were sitting outside and the rest of them agreed. Running and footsteps were approaching and the protection of the entrance groaned.

"Prophet Evdemon", I shouted in agony, and my forehead was dripping with sweat. "Prophet Evdemon."

No reply.

The grid was shaking dangerously and it wouldn't bear it. They would get in.

"Prophet Evdemon", I shouted in all my power, making him jump.

"What happened", He asked.

"They will break the entrance", I said.

"They have come again", he muttered and got out of bed. He climbed up the stairs and stood under the opening.

"They left from here", he said addressing to those standing outside.

"Are you sure they left", one of them asked.

"Yes", said the Prophet. They headed for Artikonisi. Soon, this swarm of strange warriors left with shouting and cluttering, and there was silence after a while.

"Who were these people", I asked in curiosity.

"These are the Kares warriors, looking for their men who betrayed and killed them in order to get the treasure," replied the Prophet.

"So they are pirates", I asked.

"Yes. They were tied to a tree and burned. That tree is that burnt trunk of an olive tree that has remained for such a long time next to the other olive trees. I don't know if you've seen it. Most of them made a vow to get revenge in another life before dying. So they keep on looking to get revenge to calm their soul", said the Prophet. The Prophet went down and lied down again as if nothing had happened while I was trying to calm down.

In the morning, I woke up but the Prophet wasn't in his bed. The opening of the entrance wasn't there either. Asteria was sitting and I felt bad for keeping them waiting for me. I got out and saw the Prophet on the usual top of the mountain watching the 'apodoi'. That's what they call the martins in Symi, which means 'birds with no legs', because they never sit.

The sun was high and had made even the small clouds, which were running to the North, disappear. The Prophet noticed me and approached me. When he came near me, he asked me to follow him and we went to the cave.

"It's time I told you the oracle", he said.

"I'm all ears", I said waiting.

"On the top of the island of the lepers, where God looks through the seal's eye before he leaves for his kingdom, two inches higher, dry dust should remain the iron metal. I can repeat the oracle for you a couple of times so that you will remember it", added the Prophet.

I agreed and asked him to repeat it more slowly. When he did that he said, "I am going to give you two tools which will help you in your mission in case you need them. You can choose which you want them to be." I thanked him and got out with Asteria. "On the top of the island of the lepers", said the oracle.

Which of the three islands top might that be? I would start with the big one, on which we were, and afterwards we would search the rest. We climbed up the top where the 'apodoi', which the Prophet watched, were going in and out of a hole in the rocks.

We looked for a big opening on the top but didn't find anything. We went on its other side and I was thinking of how I would go to the other islands. I should probably swim. I sat and watched, like Evdemon did, the birds going out of the hole in which they could hardly fit in. Where were they going?

There must have been a big cave underneath. That's why they enter with such force into that small hole. I searched again for a big opening but in vain. I had no idea, so I went to the place in which the birds were going in and watched them. Suddenly, I was enlightened. That hole from which the birds were going in and out was the seal's eye if you saw it from one side. In fact, that rock looked like a seal lying in the sun lazily. I ran to Asteria and announced to her my idea. That made her happy. Unfortunately there was nothing else giving me a boost to go on.

How would I enter the cave I thought was beneath us? I searched the area again more thoroughly but with no result. I was at a dead end. Unless that wasn't the seal after all. I started having doubts about my discovery and decided to swim to the second island. I said that to Asteria. She didn't object and followed me. We dived into the sea from a small beach and in a few minutes we were on the island. We climbed up to its top very quickly but unfortunately didn't find anything. That was the Artikonisi island, as Evdemon had named it. Our attempts were fruitless. There was only a small hole which no one could fit in to enter.

Feeling disappointed, I told Asteria that we would go to the small island and soon we were there. As we were climbing up, we saw an opening of a cave which was going down and then was leading to the surface. We entered and moved on in difficulty. We reached a conjunction and followed the tunnel on the right to see where it would lead us to and then we would go in the opposite direction. That tunnel was steep and full of dump.

After a while it was going down reaching a place which was by the sea. If we passed the sea, it was going up again. I dived and Asteria did the same and we swam across the other side. What we had passed was actually a big ditch between the tunnel and the sea. We moved on and on, turning when we saw an opening shed with light. That was where the route ended.

We reached the opening and I put my head in to look what was there. That opening was leading to the second island. So we went under the sea and reached Artikonisi again. There was no sign telling us that the iron metal was there. We had to return, unfortunately. We felt disappointed and our logic was at a dead end.

On our return, after the turning in the tunnel, although we knew we had to swim across it again, we realized that there was no sea anymore. Instead, there was a bottomless precipice. It was empty of water. That sight gave me the creeps and we remained looking at the abyss before us; stunned and without having neither a logical explanation nor a solution of how we would get across. We were trapped in that tunnel and there was no escape.

I decided that we should go back to that small opening in case there was a possibility for us to expand its diameter. So we went back. I took a stone and started hitting the brinks of the opening in order to remove the thinner parts of the rocks. There were times I managed it but others when I would chip the stone I was using, filling my hands with blisters. But very slowly, after hard work and trying, I managed to expand the opening so that I could get in. We now have the chance to escape from our prison.

I climbed up first and then helped Asteria to get out. We reached the middle island with the artikia again and we had to swim to the small one where the entrance of the underground tunnels were. We swam to the island and got into the tunnel knowing that the route on the right was leading to the place we had got trapped. I was sure that behind that incident with the sea disappearing, were Nohra's demons. In that way, he wanted to trap us, scare us, and warn us about what would happen next.

We were moving with great difficulty as the tunnel was getting more narrow. It had a circular diameter and on one of its turnings, some bush roots had blocked the entrance; forming a wall through which we couldn't pass. We needed a saw or an ax. They were that thick. I began to break and remove parts of the roots but obviously it would take much time and labor on my part.

I was exhausted due to my effort and the humidity. I was all sweaty and there was no ending in all this. My hands felt like they were burning. I sat down to have some rest and with the dim light there was, I discovered that some of the roots' edges were tangled up.

I was sure that it was one of Nohra's tricks again. I stood up and continued what I was doing and that time I managed to make an opening through which both Asteria and I managed to pass. As soon as we entered, it closed again. But I had no time to think about our returning. I had to move on.

The light was too faint and we didn't know where we were stepping on. So when we began feeling strong bites, first on our feet and then going up all over our body, we were terrified. I managed to catch one insect that was climbing on me, which then bit me in the finger. By touch I figured out that they were big ants which were in the tunnel.

No matter what we did, it was impossible to escape their bites. We had intruded their kingdom and their attacks aimed at sending us away from it. Unfortunately we had to suffer that torture too, as we had no other choice. Due to the fact that we couldn't see where we were stepping on, we also stumbled on stones.

The tunnel became too narrow and at some point I felt like there was no exit. By touching the wall and moving mainly having my hands to guide me, I found out that the tunnel continued on the left. As soon as we turned we saw dim light from far away. That gave me courage and I carried on with more strength. On one turn, we saw a small room on the left. As far as I could see, the ants were everywhere with large pincers and red color.

The tunnel continued and led to a brighter room. As I was examining the first room I sensed something moving on the wall opposite me. I went closer and discovered that they were two holes close to each other. In one hole I could see the head of snake and in the other its tail was hanging. That seemed to me a very weird and unconventional way for a snake to be sitting. I ignored that fact and moved on to the next room which was similar.

There was a hole high in that room from which sun rays were getting in. In the meantime the 'apodoi' kept coming in and out and I figured out the aim of their visits. They were eating the big red ants. I looked at the wall that was dividing the two rooms and saw the snake again sitting at the two holes which were the same as the other room's.

It seemed that these holes were looking through the next wall. They communicated with one another. But how did the snake turn its head? I thought of something and went back to the first room. The snake immediately turned its head going from one hole to the other. It was watching my moves. What was its role?

What impressed me was that the sun was coming through the hole on the ceiling and it was shedding light under the hole where the snake was. In that last room there were also rectangular carved stones here and there, as if someone had left them at the corner for an unknown reason. My mind had stopped. I didn't know what I should do. I brought the oracle back to my mind in hopes of finding a solution.

I recalled, "on top of the lepers' islands where God looks at through the seal's eye…" While I was thinking, the ants were keeping on with their 'work'. So if that hole from which the birds were going in and out is the seal's eye, we are now below the top of the big island.

The God's look is nothing else but the sun rays which go through it's eye. So the metal must be a couple of inches higher that the place where the sun rays shed light. But the snake was in that place, sitting in the two holes. No. No. Something was missing. Something didn't match with the facts. No matter how hard I was trying to find a solution, it was impossible.

The time was passing by and the bright spot created by the sun rays on the wall was going higher, as the sun was setting. I returned to the first room in case I found a crypt, a secret passage, but there was nothing. I went back and looked at the two holes where the snake was sitting. They were too high up for me to search for something. I also had to send the snake away.

In the meantime the bright spot from the rays was going even higher and it would soon reach one of the two holes where the snake was sitting. Something pushed me to throw a stone next to the snake to see how it would react. It immediately unrolled and came near me. I moved but it followed me. So, I went to the place where the carved stones were and threw another stone at it the moment it was about to attack me. The stone hit it on its tail and immediately the room was full of smoke as if we were in a volcano's crater; emitting smoke before the explosion of lava.

The atmosphere was suffocating. I wanted to breath but I couldn't. I wanted to go back and get some fresh air but I didn't have the strength to do it. My limbs wouldn't obey me. I was feeling weak. Asteria was next to me and she must have had the same symptoms, even though she was a bit further. I couldn't help her and neither could she help me. My legs inflected and I fainted. I opened my eyes because someone was trying to wake me up. It was Asteria.

"What happened", I asked and immediately looked at the snake. There was nothing. I looked at the sun which was coming in through the hole where the snake had been sitting before. Something flashed in my mind. I stood up and ran to the other room. The ray was going through the hole towards the wall of the next room. I thought that the metal would be a bit higher. It was too high for me to reach.

I brought three or four stones and placed the one onto the other. I climbed up to the spot where the ray was and counted two inches. I couldn't see anything. I hit it with my hand but still nothing. I was so angry that I started hitting it at the same place until I was in pain and stopped. I stood up on my toes and searched higher but the stone on which I was standing moved and to avoid falling down, I held on to a stone which was on my right. A noise was heard and I saw a hole in the wall.

I put my hand in and removing a few pieces from the opening I made it wider and then I discerned a marble box. With my hands shaking from thrill and excitement, I made the opening even wider and took it in my hands and climbed down the stones. "Asteria", I shouted, "we have found it"!

She came and we opened the box which was full of red dust. It was the iron metal. I took the sacred pot made of alabaster and filled it with the dust glowing from joy for the outcome. I put it in the bag I was carrying and made our way back after putting the box and stones back to their place.

On our way back, what impressed us was that the roots of the trees weren't there anymore. They had disappeared. We got out of the opening and dived in the water. I was holding the bag with the valuable load, which was putting an end on my fourth test, really tight.

We arrived at the big island and I ran to the Prophet full of joy to announce him the news. He was happy and asked to see the iron dust. I took the sacred pot out of my leather bag and when I opened it I shouted in surprise. I couldn't believe my eyes. The dust had been dissolved into the sea while we were swimming. I couldn't imagine I would be that unlucky.

"That's why I asked you to show it to me", said Evdemon. "Can you imagine what would happen if you discovered that after leaving from here?" I was about to cry. I didn't have the courage to go through all of it again. I sat on a stone and started thinking what I would do. Nohra and his demons must have laughed at me that moment and discussed what they would do next. What obstacles and disasters they would cause to discourage me even more.

I stood up and searched around. Without anything to sail on, I wouldn't be able to bring back the dust dry. So I needed a boat. And since there wasn't one, I had to make it on my own. That was the only solution. I had to make it for another reason too. For our returning from the islands of the lepers in Symi. I remembered what the Prophet had told me. He would give me two tools when I would need them. So the tools I would ask from him would be a saw and a knife. Evdemon brought them to me and I started working.

I took the saw, cut a large piece of cedar and then with a knife I carved strips at the size of a finger on its edge and in that way I had a kind of rope. When I finished I took out four-five strips and then cut another branch in order to do the same. So I had ten strips from that offhand rope which could help me make a raft that would transfer us from the islands of the lepers. But the cedars were heavy. I had to think of another way. The artikia would be more ideal because they were lighter and easier to cut.

I took the strips, joined them and tied them around my waist. Asteria didn't need any as I would go to Artikonisi on my own to bring the artikia I needed. I dived into the sea and soon I was on the island. I started immediately. I was cutting the dry trunks of the artikia and piled them up. When I finished, I had eight packs that could fit in my arms. I tied them together with the ropes I had made before. Then I got on and using an artiki as an oar, I managed to reach the big island. I had many thing to do there but it was getting dark. I pulled the packs one by one and transferred them to the island. I tied them around the cedars in case there was wind and I planned what I would do the following day.

I was thinking all night how I would build the raft. It had to be strong and able to get us not only to the small island but to Symi as well. One possible solution would be to make two long and narrow cylinders and adjust a grid made of cedar on them;

on which we would sit so that we would be two inches far from the sea surface.

The best would be to place a mast and I would ask Evdemon to give me a piece of cloth which I would use as a sail in order to make our trip to Symi shorter. I would also have two oars for security. My eyes closed and I left the rest for the following day. I would see what I would do.

It was the first time I would use all of the three days I had at my disposal. I didn't expect things would turn out that way. I got to work very early in the morning. I cut ten long branches , the straightest I could find, which were four meters long and another ten, which were two meters long, in order to place them vertically and make the grid.

I removed the strips from the branches as they were necessary for tying. then I took the artikia joined them in order to make two big packs in the shape of a cylinder which I tied together very tightly. The whole success of my raft depended on their durability. I tied the grid on them and built a raft which looked like a catamaran. I felt like Ulysses with my construction with the durability of which my test would be successful.

I finally searched and found four more trees; the straightest there were. I would use one as a mast, another one to place it vertically on the mast and two more as oars. I fixed the mast at the center after having passed its edge until it found a vertical piece of wood, which I had placed by joining with its two, edges the middle of the cylinders.

While I was working, I was thinking of how I would ask the Prophet for the piece of cloth that I needed as a sail. When I finished, Asteria was still sitting there, watching with interest what I was trying to do and Prophet Evdemon was still watching the 'apodous'. When he came down, he had an announcement to make.

"The birds", he said, "have stopped going in and out of the hole, which is weird."

"And what does this mean", I asked very curious.

"If I interpret it correctly, something must have scared them. There is something underground which they sense," he said.

"What can this be", I replied.

"I don't know, but the birds are so innocent creatures. Only something bad can scare them and make them change their habits", said the Prophet.

"Maybe the ants which they eat have hidden", I said.

He replied, "no, it's not that. It must be something else."

I felt a pain in my stomach. Was something even worse expecting me? Who knows! The day was about to end and with the construction of the raft I didn't have time to try and get the metal again. So I left it for the following day.

At night the cave was lit up by an oil lamp and the stories of Evdemon together with my experiences and trials were filling the atmosphere. I learnt something there which really impressed me. Evdemon told me that the island of Symi had over two hundred caves and underground precipices. In other words my island was like a sponge.

One example was the islands that were connected underground through the tunnels. In these underground caves all the chthonic and malicious creatures found shelter and a place to hide as the sun light could kill and exterminate them. That's why they were hiding in the dark lurking for an unlucky man who would make the mistake and enter their world.

How many times had I entered the caves to play as a kid! There was always something cold, something frightening in those visits. Now I know why. The underground spirits were there, though I couldn't see them at the time. They were waiting for the right opportunity to make their presence understood.

I remember one day I tried to climb down a small cliff with another child older than me. When we were returning, my friend had climbed up but I couldn't. I was at the opening of the cliff half a meter before the ground's surface with my legs open but I didn't have the strength to move my leg. Something was pulling me down with incredible force. My legs were shaking and I wanted to let myself free-fall rather than make a step up. I had the same feeling during my trial at Dysalonas.

Before I slept, I thought about every single detail of the next day's attempt. Unfortunately though, many times you make plans but things happen differently. The sun hadn't risen yet. Asteria was out inspecting the raft and Evdemon was at his usual place at the top. Someone had to help me bring the raft to the sea. If I told this to Asteria, would she help me or would she regard this as a breach of duty?

I asked her and she nodded and went to one edge of the raft to help lift. We took the raft in our hands and threw it into the sea. I was so anxious to see how it would 'react'. I boarded first and then I helped Asteria board too. It was steady and seemed to be bearing our weight. I took one oar and by rowing left and right we managed to get to the small island.

She helped me pull the raft out of the water and stopped for a while before entering the cave, thinking of what was expecting me. We got in and moved forward through the conjunction as we had done the previous time. After we had passed by the place where we had seen the roots, we saw a blue light or to be exact, many blue lights which appeared to be coming towards us.

At the same time I heard a voice in my mind:

> "Did you think that your mission was over?
> You are mistaken. Nothing is gained without
> pain. Nothing is gained without something
> in return. You have to give something. You
> left like a thief the other time, and thought
> that you had gotten what you wanted. You
> still haven't gotten it and you won't get it as
> long as I am here. So I'm sending you the
> Polyakanthos in order to give it what I must
> take as an exchange for your life. It had been
> waiting in the dark for centuries and it's
> time to get to know my power through it."

It's Nohra, I thought to myself. That was him.

In the meantime, the light was getting closer and I
saw a strange creature which I hadn't seen before
even in my dreams. It was coming from the depths
of the darkest powers of Nohra and his thirst for
revenge from those who don't obey him.

It was basically a ball with long spines like a sea-
urchin, and with tentacles shorter than the spines
like moving threads. All the edges of the tentacles
were shining and they were giving out a blue light.
As far as I understood these tentacles must have
been his eyes. The spines were black in their base
becoming purple as they were going up leading to
their edges which were white. They were the same
size as the tunnels opening so I couldn't move

forward without confronting it first. It was inevitable.

But how on Earth could I fight a monster since I had nothing to hit it with except for my hands? Would I have to fight an enormous sea-urchin with bare hands? The big sea-urchin came closer to me and if I hadn't moved back, its spines would have pricked me. Asteria had stayed a bit behind waiting to see the outcome of my fighting with the monster.

I was obliged to go back and think about what I had to do. It followed me and I moved towards the exit. Soon, the multi-tentacled monster arrived. I was wondering how long I would wait. Time was running and I didn't have the luxury to waste it because I didn't have only to fill the sacred pot with the iron dust but I also had to return with the raft and I didn't know how all this would work.

I thought of sticking onto the tunnel's walls to see what it would do. It moved coming close to me, I felt its spines pricking my left leg and arm. I screamed because I was in pain. On a final, desperate attempt to stop it, I touched one of its bright tentacles that were moving before me, and pulled it with all the strength I had which was multiplied by my fear and the pain.

A sound was heard like when you open a bottle and the tentacle remained in my hand. I threw it in disgust. Its light faded and it started shrinking until all that remained was something like a deflated balloon spilling out all the liquid it had inside. My left arm and leg were bleeding but that made me more determined. I had to find a way to finish with that.

If I had something like a shield, a piece of wood or something else that would protect me, I would be able to fight it. I moved back searching in the tunnel with the monster following me. There was a curve at a point and then I found the solution I was looking for. I got in there and waited.

The monster came but its spines couldn't reach me in the curve I was in. But I had the chance to pull out another tentacle until I removed ten of them. The monster, after each removal of a tentacle, was moving back and then returned with the side he had the more tentacles so that he could see me. That way, without wanting it, it enabled me to blind it gradually.

After much time had passed, there were only three or four tentacles left before I would blind it completely. When I removed the last one it started shrinking making a sound like a siren, until all that was left was a small ball. Nothing had happened to its spines but other than that it didn't have any signs of being alive. Then, I touched a spine and pushed it down with force and broke it like a piece of dry wood. I had found the way to disarm it.

After I had broken the ones that were blocking my way out, I broke those on the right and made space for us to pass and reach the room with the metal. After much effort and exhaustion, I made a way for us to pass through. I also took one of the spines to use it as a weapon in case we needed it. It was a little thinner than my wrist.

Without any more obstacles, we arrived at the first room where the crypt with the marble box was that had the iron dust inside. We saw nothing worrying. I got the dust and put it in the sacred pot and headed for the exit. As we were going out, I took another spine as a token of the monster.

We got on the raft being careful with the metal's dust. Then the phrase of the oracle came to my mind: 'the iron metal should dry dust should remain dry dust', which I hadn't interpreted correctly before.

We arrived at the island and Evdemon was waiting for us at the beach. He looked at the two loot-spines of Polyakanthos with great interest and examined them carefully. It was time for us to go as it was the final day of that test and I didn't know what difficulties we would face on our returning.

What I did was cut another four small cedar branches and tie them round the gaps between the pieces of wood in order to make the mast stronger.

"Prophet Evdemon", I said, "I want to thank you for your help and I would like to meet you again if it's logically possible."

He gave me an enigmatic smile and said, "nothing is impossible for people anymore. After creating God until he could tame the earth, now what remains is to become God in God's place."

There was silence and I was fighting with my lack of courage to ask for a piece of cloth that I wanted him to give me. In the end, Evdemon left for the cave and I was left behind with my wish. After a while he appeared again and I couldn't believe my eyes. He was holding the piece of cloth in his hands.

"Take this with you to put it in the raft and sit on it", he said.

There were no words for me to thank him for what he did. I supposed he had guessed my wish getting me out of my dilemma. After I had organized everything, we set off but I didn't place the sail as there wasn't any wind. So, I took the oars and we started receding from the islands of the lepers.

After a while a breeze started blowing and I decided to adjust the mast. It wasn't easy but by removing the thread from the textile, I managed to place it tying it up with it. As we were sailing, I was looking at Asteria who was suffering so much with me only because she had to supervise and be present during my tests.

What has she done to deserve being tortured with me? As I was looking at her, I was trying to remember where I had seen her before, provided of course I remembered correctly. There couldn't be logic in such an absurd occurrence in time where the reality was mixed with fantasy in an endless game of prevalence.

We were in the middle of the route when two huge fish appeared near us in looking like dolphins having black color. We were happy because we thought we would have company but soon we changed our mind. The dolphins weren't actually dolphins as we thought and with their first hits against the artikia we almost fell into the sea.

Moreover the artikia weren't strong like wood so they couldn't bear the hitting. We also hadn't tied the raft with real ropes but with the strips from the cedar. That meant I had to do something really fast before the next hit was catastrophic. I raised one branch which I was using as an oar in order to hit one of the fish that was coming from the right side, but the fish from left side hit us instead.

Asteria fell into the sea and I pulled her up by giving her the oar. I was searching for solutions and suddenly I noticed the two big spines of Polyakanthos which I had tied on the mast as a souvenir. I untied them quickly and took one, praying to God to help me aim properly.

The fish on the left attacked us again and I was waiting for the right moment to hit it. When it came closer, I threw the one and a half- meter spine with all the power I had, pointing at its eyes. The spine was pinned near its eye but due to its force, it hit the raft again and as result it broke two or three artikia.

That was a negative course but at least we had one enemy less. The hurt devil's fish was trying to free from the spine by turning and moving over the sea's surface but in vain. Soon, we saw blood on the surface which was a sign that the spine had produced good results.

The second fish tried to hit us from behind but due to its rage for revenge, it got stuck between the cylinders of the artikia and that was a good chance for me to hit it while it was immobilized.

Indeed, I managed to hit it between its eyes and even though it tried hard to escape, it was hitting only its tail making the raft run fast as if it had an engine. When it stopped hitting the raft, proof that it was dead, we were facing the problem of stopping the raft from sinking because of the fish's weight.

I took the bag with the sacred pot out, gave it to Asteria to keep it and I jumped into the water with the oar on my hand. I started hitting the fish at the front side until I finally managed to dislodge it and let it sink into the deep waters, taking the spine with it.

I got on the raft, which was tipping on its left side due to the breaking of the artikia and had lost its steadiness. We had to sit on one side to balance it and continued our voyage with no problems.

We arrived at the port from which we had left three days ago. We left the raft and headed for the Temple of Karnios Apollo at the old Daphniei settlement. The sun was setting to the west when we arrived at the temple and everything had a sweet rosy appearance.

Mystic Melas was standing at the entrance gazing at the west when he noticed us coming up. He smiled and when we stood in front of him he said, "you have succeeded in persuading us that you don't give up no matter how many obstacles stand in your way, he said addressing to me, that's why you deserve to be called 'tireless gladiator'".

I thanked him and gave him the pot with the dust of the iron metal.

"It's time", he said, "you initiated in some of the God's secrets", without giving another explanation. I nodded and as we were leaving we met Aetion who was coming.

So, the three of us set off our return.

Chapter 21

I had completed more than half of my tests which gave me hope for my return and strength to go on. What I didn't understand from Mystic Mela's last words, was his phrase 'It's time you initiated in some of the God's secrets'. What secrets? I hope this doesn't mean more problems and trouble for me.

There were three tests left and I would free myself from that invisible world and get back to reality. But something was scaring me. Something didn't give me the certainty that it would happen. Maybe it was because of the mysticism of the Mystics and the people of Okria, or the faceless behavior of Asteria, or Nohra's machinations, intriguing and rage for revenge because I rejected his proposals and was objecting to his plans. Because of all these reasons, I didn't know what to expect next. I would still be trying with all my power to get of that place no matter what price I would pay.

Chapter 22

We returned from the Temple of Karnios Apollo and we were so tired that I lay down to rest my limbs which needed that rest more than anything. I banished these thoughts out of my mind and let sleep fill every gap in a sweet way; with rest and silence as balsam to my tiredness. I woke up when I heard knocking on the door. I asked who it was and Aetion answered. I opened the door and he was waiting for me to learn about the mission.

"What mission", I asked. I thought that the next test will be performed in three days.

"Yes", he replied. "This mission is about an initiation ceremony that will take place at the Temple of Miragetis Apollo by Hyperinor."

There was silence. What initiation was that? I thought. I shut the door behind me and we left. We followed the familiar way we had walked the first time I had visited the temple.

Hyperinor was sitting at the center of the Temple's chamber and the Priests were forming a circle around him standing up. They had been waiting for me as I understood. With a gesture he showed me that I should go in front of the God's statue. I went there and he asked me to touch it with my hands and kneel down.

When I did that he said:

> "You have shown a remarkable courage and persistence and God will provide you with another weapon - equipment against Nohra and his demons. Today, he continued, you will acquire with God's grace the power to have authority over the demons once in a year but not more than once in one day.

> You are given this grace because the tests will get more difficult and you will have to be strong in order to deal with them; and also as a reward for all you have been through so far. You will repeat what you will hear declaimed by the Priestess and then it will be given to you written on a piece of leather in case you forget it later."

When the Priestess began declaiming, I didn't understand a thing of what she was saying but I was repeating faithfully what I was hearing.

'NROB YB EHT NUS DOG OLLOPA, OHW NAC EKAM EHT KRAD RAEPPASID HTIW RUOY THGIL, DEHS RUOY YAR DNA EVIG RUOY REWOP OT RUOY LAYOL REVEILEB

OHW SEKOVNI UOY OT EZILIBOMMI SIH SEIMENE ECNO NI YTINRETE'.

Hyperinor was right to tell me about the leather on which this code was written. It would have been impossible for me to remember all these difficult key words.

My fingertips that were touching the statue felt so hot as if they had caught fire. As if God's statue wasn't made of marble, but of hot coal. The declaim had finished but Hyperinor remained silent, praying. Then he stood up and nodded. A Priestess brought a small piece of leather in which the initiation code was written and gave it to Hyperinor. The Priestesses slowly left and I was alone with Mystic.

"Well", I heard Hyperinor's voice in my mind saying. "Look at him".

I unfolded the leather and saw what was declaimed written there. I still couldn't understand a thing.

"You can declaim that, the voice in mind was heard again, and Nohra's demons will be immobilized immediately for a moment", he said.

"But I don't understand what it is saying", I replied.

"If you want to learn its hidden meaning, you can read it to yourself but silently, beginning backwards", he said.

So I began reading it backwards and to my surprise I understood its hidden meaning.

'BORN BY THE SUN GOD APOLLO, WHO CAN MAKE THE DARK DISAPPEAR WITH YOUR LIGHT, SHED YOUR RAY AND GIVE YOUR POWER TO YOUR LOYAL BELIEVER WHO INVOKES YOU TO IMMOBILIZE HIS ENEMIES ONCE IN ETERNITY'.

"The initiation is completed", said Hyperinor aloud. "What you heard will remain here."

I nodded and he showed me the exit. I thanked him, made a curtsy and departed. I found Aetion outside waiting for me. We headed for Okria and I was holding the valuable weapon from the God, with a pain in my stomach from what was awaiting me.

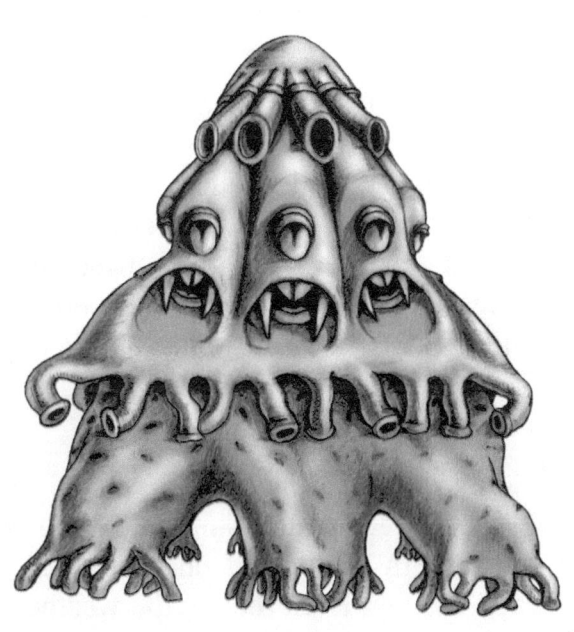

Chapter 23

WET GRAVE

After I had taken Apollo's code, I tried to learn it by heart because I didn't know when I would need it. There were times when I reminisced about my home again and my life so far. I was looking for the causes that brought me here. But there were no answers.

On one hand, what was happening to me was absurd, and on the other hand if it hadn't happened to me and someone told me that it would, I would have thought he was crazy. Unfortunately, there was no way I could react unless I carried out all the tests successfully. But that required patience and persistence. The days went by fast and it was time for my Fifth test. Aetion reminded me of it when he came to accompany me.

We picked Asteria up again and walked along a road which was leading to a summit. At the summit we could discern a block of buildings lost in the clouds and the fog. Even though the weather down in Okria was different, up here the climate was different; as if we were in another season as soon as we arrived. Our clothes were sticking on our body due to humidity and we could hardly breathe.

The Temple had a large and high yard and it was built with brown and light green stones which were creating a kind of mosaic. The temple was extending on the top and I thought that during winter time it must be difficult to live there due to the weather conditions. In front of the building one of the many names of Apollo, to whom the temple was dedicated, was written - Ulios.

A priest guided us to the Mystic who was dressed in white and was discussing with other priests about the the yard of the Temple, if I understood correctly. As soon as he saw us, he sent the other priests away and Aetion left us alone.

"I am Mystic Krantor", he introduced himself, "and the metal I want you to bring to me, is lead. It requires much thought and attention", he went on, "in order for you to carry out this test successfully. Your meeting with Nohra's demons will be inevitable."

There was silence and only the wind was heard blowing on the top. Then Mystic Krantor said:

> "The oracle for this trial is the following: 'On the west of the island, at Lappatos Bay, under the bottom of the sea, in the wet grave

of thirty-three demons who were enclosed there by Hyperinor, in seven shells, is the metal. There is one entrance in one mouth of the Earth on land and another at the center of the bay under the triangle between two erect rocks."

Everything seemed very confusing to me but what terrified me was that the metal was where thirty three of Nohra's demons also were. Mystic Krantor was quiet after the oracle and crossed his hands in front of him. I turned and looked toward Asteria who was waiting to see what would happen.

Krantor left from the place where he was sitting and saying 'follow me' he got into the Temple. We ran behind him and he stood in front of the God's statue, whispering a secret prayer. Then he addressed to us saying, "take the pot made of amethyst to put the metal into you'll get from the Fifth test."

We took the pot, bowed and got out. I was feeling very weird. I didn't know where to begin. And why were there two entrances, on in the land and one in the sea? One of the two would be easier to reach, I thought. But which? Since we were on land I should try from this entrance, first.

Which is the mouth of the Earth? I wondered. It must be either a precipice or a cave. But where was it? Where was Asteria going? Was she going there?

"Are we going to the entrance", I asked her and she nodded. What would we do if we needed rope?

I was moving forward without talking. The thoughts about the test which I had to go through and the difficulties I would face, were torturing me. I was sure that it wouldn't be easy. Apollo's code came to mind, which gave me the possibility to immobilize the demons for a moment. I repeated it silently to myself to remember it.

In fact, I had some queries about how long would that 'moment' be that was mentioned in the text last, so I asked Aetion. His answer was the following: from the moment you finish reading the code, you have as much time as the time you need to say the twelve most popular names of Apollo: Lycios, Numinios, Evdomagetis, Thargilios, Miragetis, Voidromios, Smithephs, Parnopios, Alexikakos, Carnios, Agitor, Ulios.

We had gotten into a gorge with really steep rocks on which cypresses had grown. We walked with great difficulty while five or six corvus cornixes were croaking and their voices were echoing. Suddenly, someone behind us was heard shouting. I stood and listened carefully.

"Wait for me", he was heard saying.

I looked at Asteria who also looked in wonder.

"Who can it be", I asked her.

She answered by making a sign that she didn't know. We waited but nobody showed up so we decided to proceed.

"Wait for me", he was heard again. "I am a human too."

"Come", I shouted being curious of seeing who he was. We waited for him again but nothing.

I could see that something was going wrong. So I decided that we should leave without waiting for him and I wouldn't answer if I heard the voice again. I started saying the prayer secretly to myself.

But I didn't wait have to wait long to realize that something was actually going wrong. A sudden strong wind started blowing; drifting everything. It uprooted bushes, broke branches of trees and created a 'ball' which was running; lifting dust, rolling even stones. In the meantime, I could hear curses and screams coming from that 'ball' which gave me the creeps.

"Hold on tight to the trunk", I screamed to Asteria, and I did the same. We held onto a big cypress while the whirlwind was whipping us all over, hurting our bodies with the objects that were thrown at us. It wanted to lift us from the ground and throw us down and break us like small twigs onto the rocks. The atmosphere was full of leaves and dust creating a nightmarish scenery.

When the wind settled down everything looked like having been bombarded. The trees had no leaves and their trunks were full of holes. There was a freezing silence all around as if every living creature had disappeared from the area while our mouths had a taste of dust and earth.

Our bodies hurt in the parts where that whirlwind had hit us and they were full of bruises and scars. We shook the dust and leaves from our body and sat down to come round from that weird outburst of Nohra's demons. They had caused that. There was no doubt about it.

Then we moved forward and turned left. The Lappatos bay appeared and it would take us approximately a hundred meters to get to the beach. We turned left again and suddenly we came across a precipice on the edges of which osiers had grown. I looked at the depth and realized that it was deepening at levels which we could pass if we tried. I didn't know what to anticipate afterwards.

I climbed up an osier, held onto a branch, and let my body sway in order to reach the first level. Then, I waited for Asteria to do the same and with a little help she did it. I made some thoughts with this contact between us – it was the second time after the test at Nanou in the sea - which I pushed away as soon as possible.

We went down at another level and our descending was easier. There wasn't much light and a whisper was heard. It was undefined. It was something like growling, high-pitched voices which was getting louder as we were going near. I stopped and the noise was more intense now. It seemed that we would meet it really soon.

A black cloud that kept changing in thickness and size was coming fast causing pandemonium from the shouts. When we were hit by this swarm I realized that they were bats.

"Lie down prostrate", I said to Asteria and I did the same.

It took the bats much time to get out and some them left their signature on us. Some on our back, feet. We were filled with scratches and bites. I looked at the dim light at Asteria who had the same scars as me and I felt sorry for her.

But what could I do? It didn't depend on me to make it stop. On the other hand I was the reason why all these things were happening to her. However the situation was, I still felt really bad but I didn't have the ability to change the situation. I should either stop the tests and remain a spirit or carry them out with Asteria suffering with me.

Life is full of dilemmas, I thought. You spend a whole life searching for a grain of happiness without finding it. I stopped my introspection and nodded to Asteria to go on. Time was valuable.

We moved on and the air smelled of mold and moisture. We must have descended under the sea level. We reached the end and there was nothing to show us that the route continued. There was a wall of rocks before us and in its center I could discern a pattern on the biggest boulder. I went nearer and recognizes the symbol of Okria carved on it. Behind that must be the thirty three demons of Nohra who were imprisoned by Hyperinor.

There was no possibility I could do anything from that point. It was obvious. We had to leave and try from the side of the sea. I told Asteria and she agreed with me. That wall couldn't be demolished even if you hit it really hard and neither could you move a rock to open a passage. The secret key that opened it was something else but I couldn't think of anything.

I left disappointed and with my head full of thoughts. We started our return. Fortunately, on our returning, nothing happened and we got onto the surface safely. Now we had to go to the beach and dive into the sea for the second entrance.

We dived and I started seeking at the centre, as the oracle said. Nothing. I didn't trace anything that looked like what it said. I went to the center of the beach again, and started looking. Then I saw two rocks at the bottom of the sea and showed them to Asteria. I dived and went closer.

It wasn't very deep. I estimated at about four meters. Two big rocks were fixed into the bottom of the sea; one opposite the other with a distance of one fathom between them. Nothing else. We could see no entrance between them in the bottom.

I went onto the surface to breath and Asteria was waiting for me. I dived again, and went to the bottom again between the two rocks and searched with my hand. There was sand which was stirred up with my movement, blurring the water. I went to the surface and waited for the water to clear and when the sand settled, I discerned a piece of stone at the point where I had searched with my hand.

I dived again and tried to understand its size. It was triangular but I couldn't lift it. It seemed to be quite heavy. I got on the surface again to take the necessary breaths and tried to move it by pushing it from one side. It moved a bit. I felt encouraged and carried on.

I pushed it a little bit more to get it out of the centre between the rocks and then I saw a hole as big as a nut. I looked at it in disappointment if that was the entrance that the oracle meant. Then I saw bubbles coming out taking shape. Only then did I realize what they were becoming.

These bubbles were the bodiless demons which were escaping through the entrance and they were forming in the water. If they got onto the surface, I wouldn't be able to see them neither confront them. How can you fight an enemy that you can't see?

I had only one chance to see them in the sea. I ran as fast as I could and closed the opening by pulling the triangular stone onto it. One of the bodiless demons had already been shaped and began attacking me.

He wanted to keep me underwater so that I would run out of air and he was pulling me down non-stop. Even if I escaped from him, at times he was in charge. Whenever I managed to go onto the surface, he was pulling me from my feet to drown me.

I couldn't cope with just one demon, I thought, how would I cope with thirty two more? I didn't even want to imagine that scenario. I was fighting now. Fighting for my life.

It seemed that the many years of staying down there in the wet cave of Hyperinor, had made them very aggressive , ready to get revenge because of all that they had been through because of him. I couldn't find a solution and the exhaustion made my body heavy from my trying to remain on the surface.

Asteria was looking at my titanic fight against the demon, in fright, not being able to interfere and I was fighting for a few breaths of oxygen. At those moments I brought back to memory similar situations.

When I was little, I remember we went swimming with my family and I was wearing a life jacket. But it got untied and fell off me and I was trying desperately to stay on the surface due to the instinct of self-preservation. I was fighting with all my power because I didn't know how to swim. Fortunately, my father was near and jumped into the sea with his clothes on and got me ashore. Since then my mother celebrated that day. I had the same feeling. The same agony to stay on the surface.

Apollo's code flashed into my mind and I started reciting it as soon as I got onto the surface for a second. I didn't manage to say it all and the demon pulled me down to the bottom of the sea. However, I didn't stop saying it even into the sea, making bubbles with every word until I finally said it all.

The demon stayed still underwater and I got onto the surface with all the power I was left with and I called Asteria, "swim fast to the shore", and I started.

Swimming as fast as we could, we went ashore and I lay on the beach feeling exhausted. I was almost unconscious. Now I had to think how I would fight with all the demons who wanted to get revenge through me for their imprisonment into the cave. I had no chance to outdo them. The one entrance from the land was closed, the other one from the sea unapproachable. So what was left for me? Give up?

No. This shouldn't happen. I had gone through half of the tests already and I didn't have the right in my conscience to think that way. There must have been a solution. Normally, what I had to do first, was get the bodiless demons out of the cave. But how would that happen without touching them?

I had an idea. If I inserted into the hole a pot from the opposite side, I would gather them all in there. But how would I transfer them afterwards? It was good as a thought but it was difficult to put it into practice. I needed a different material. Another object. Whatever I did I had to go back and work it out so that I would get the ideal tool.

I told Asteria that we were going back to Okria because I couldn't find a solution at that moment. We were returning, not from the gorge this time because we didn't want to pass from the precipice, but through an ordinary path.

On our way back at some point, we heard music coming from a small house made of dry stone wall, like the one shepherds play. I stood to listen to that monotonous slow sound produced by the 'touloumi' as the Symiots call the skinbag (a musical instrument made of goatskin). Magnetized by the music I headed for the house without thinking about it.

I was almost there when two sheepdogs attacked me barking in threatening way. I stood still so as not to provoke them and soon the shepherd appeared at the door and calmed them down with a whistle. They smelled me and then went back. So I took the courage to go nearer.

I greeted him and said that I was lured by the music he was playing. He smiled and invited me in to listen to him from close. I called Asteria who was left behind and we all got into the house.

It was a very small house, inconvenient. A bed made of stones, two stools and a small table, was all the furniture it had. The equipment needed for his animals were more. 'Tsambalia' (bells) in different sizes, tools for the making of milk and cheese, 'katsounades' (shepherd's crooks) to catch the animals, collars, elaborate leather charms with fringes and colorful beads hanging from them.

There was also another 'touloumi' like the one he was playing, along with a few cups and earthenware jars for milk and water. He was waiting for me to look around the house's interior and our eyes met, he smiled at me and said, "would you like to hear the hymn for the 'Pan' (God of Nature, the Wild, Shepherds, Flocks, Goats, of Mountain Wilds, and is often associated with sexuality)?"

"I would be delighted to listen to whatever you play", I said and sat on a stool.

The sound was slow in the beginning, like a crying for the hardships of a shepherd's life, and made the dogs fall into sleep like a lullaby. The shepherd's voice was rough like the stones and was heard throughout the room every time he accompanied his music; narrating his monotonous life away from other people with only his animals for company.

Then the music became faster, as he was singing about fairies of the forest and the Pan who was running among the trees followed by his troupe. I had gotten so carried away that I forgot the reason why was there. But when I remembered I shouted so loudly that I made the shepherd stop at the point where the music was becoming even faster following the dance of Pan.

"Don't stop", I shouted. "Go on." And I stood up and started dancing to the rhythm of the 'touloumi' following the steps of Pan. I had found the solution for dealing with the demons and it was a good chance to dance and celebrate it.

The shepherd was playing the 'touloumi' more joyfully and since there wasn't a song but only melody, he played it even faster. I was jumping like a lunatic from joy as if I was under the influence of Dionysus. The shepherd stopped playing because I was out of breath, but I went on dancing. When I stopped, I felt very dizzy. I was stumbling until I finally managed to balance.

"You were bewitched by the music of Pan", said the shepherd.

"That's for sure", I said. "That musical instrument is blessed. I would really love to learn how to play it."

"I can teach you some of the secrets of playing the 'touloumi'", he said.

I replied, "I would love to."

Then he said, "and because I can see how enthusiastic you are with it, I tell you with all my heart that I can give you one because I have two."

"I will accept it with all my pleasure", I replied.

"Here. Take it", he said, and unhooked his second 'touloumi' from the wooden crotch where it was hanging from. I took it to my hands with yearning while Asteria was watching us; really surprised with my behavior, as I understood from the look on her face.

After thanking him, I asked him if he had any rope because I needed it. He stood up and took from a corner a ball of leather string which is called 'sirimi'.

"This one", he said, "is very strong and is made of goat leather which we process for a long time. You can see that it's thin but if you try to cut it, you can't", he added.

Indeed, I tried and it felt really strong.

"Do it with more strength", he said.

I tried to prove that it wasn't that strong but I finally admitted that nothing could break that leather strip. There was no way you could cut it.

"Take as much as you want", he said.

I measured one fathom and he cut it with a knife. I didn't know how to thank him enough. I went near him, hugged him and told him how grateful I was for all that he had done for me. He smiled widely and with a gesture he showed him that it was nothing for him. I said goodbye to him and as I was going out of the house I noticed a bronze nail on the floor. I took it because it might be proved useful.

"Let's go to the beach", I said to Asteria who was still looking at me in wonder without being able to understand my behavior and attitude.

We went to the beach and I started seeking. I wanted to find a reed at the diameter of the entrance under the triangular stone. The sea throws out pieces of wood and reeds especially during winter time so I found a lot of them very quickly. I chose the strongest and I carved it with the nail in order to cut it in uniform length.

Then I cut by carving many times with all my strength the 'touloumi's leather at the point where the musician blew to play it, estimating that the reed I had chosen would fit in. Then I passed through the reed and took the strong leather string and wrapped from the outside the leather at the point where I had passed the reed and then tied it really tight. Then I took the string and closed the little openings where the musician put his fingers for the notes and so I had the skinbag which was open only from the side where the reed was. I had the tool I needed now.

I explained to Asteria what I was thinking of doing with it but I asked her to help me because without her contribution I wouldn't be able to carry out this test. She seemed to hesitate. I know she had taken an oath not to interfere nor help me in my tests. But I told her that any kind of help would be in favor of eliminating the demons and our fight was constant for all of us. Besides, like in Nanou, she had helped me dispense from the fish and I owed her gratitude till that day but I hadn't mentioned it to anyone; nor would I mention anything about that now.

She tried to say something but she couldn't and turned her face to avoid my look. But I was waiting for an answer and insisted. When she looked at me there were tears on her cheeks. I felt guilty again like the first time I found out that she was mute.

"I'm sorry if I have made you feel uncomfortable. I won't insist more. I know that you suffer a great deal because of me but it's not something that I want. It isn't up to my power. The only thing I can do is thank you for going through all this by my side," I said.

I tried to leave but she held my hand and nodded, which meant that she would help me. I wanted to hug her to express my gratitude but I didn't know what she would think of that. So I just thanked her again and we set off.

I had thought of all the details and I repeated them to Asteria so that we wouldn't make a mistake. Asteria swam with me holding the goatskin and when we reached the two rocks we prepared ourselves psychologically and I gave the signal to dive.

I took the triangular stone right away and pushed it and as soon as the hole appeared, Asteria inserted the reed and secured it. Then I got onto the surface to take a few breaths and dived to take Asteria's place and hold the goatskin. Every time one of us who was at the bottom of the sea ran out of oxygen, we raised our hand in order to change position with the other. By doing this we gathered the demons into the goatskin.

After I had estimated - because of the time that had passed and the size of the goatskin - that they were all in, I tied it with the leather string and took it on the surface in triumph.

"We've made it", I shouted as if I had already taken the lead metal but I had to go to the precipice's entrance again to see how I would go through that wall that Hyperinor had created in order to close them in.

We got out to the beach feeling exhausted by our constant diving into the sea and I was really happy for the outcome. But if it hadn't been for Asteria, I wouldn't have been able to imprison the demons into the goatskin. This was still a secret between us though, which I would keep from everyone.

We set off after a while and got in through the precipice's entrance and I was thinking of how I would overcome the obstacle of the wall. We were nearly at the end of our route, me at the front holding the goatskin with the bodiless demons and Asteria behind me. Suddenly I felt that my feet were in water.

What happened, I thought to myself. Has a passage opened causing the sea to get in or was it another trick of Nohra? Eventually, the wall with Okria's symbol wasn't there anymore. It seems that now that the demons weren't in the cave anymore, it had no reason to exist.

I proceeded in the cave and discerned on its walls a settlement of testacea which are called 'garipodes' in Symi and as soon as they sensed our presence they got into their shell. It's hard to open them even after you have removed them from the rocks, which you can do only by using a lath-hammer. But I had the suitable tool.

I looked carefully where the largest opening on the shell was, and I was sticking the nail into it making them open because of the pain. I started searching them carefully, which required a lot of effort because the water was covering me in the cave so I had to go onto the surface in order to breathe.

I picked seven lead nuggets from each shell that were kept there like pearls. I could finally say that I had finished that test too. I didn't leave the goatskin from my hands and I had tied it around my hand for security. I searched for Asteria but I couldn't see her anywhere.

"Asteria", I shouted, but got no reply.

Has something bad happened to her? I thought. I screamed her name again, but in vain. I decided to head from the entrance, since Asteria wasn't there, and I had completed the mission. I was wandering with a heavy heart for her luck and when I got to the entrance, I raised my head and saw her.

Oh my God! She was hanging from her thick hair on the osier with a sad, complaining look in her eyes. The demons had probably lifted her and tied her with her hair and she was afraid of moving in fear of falling down. I was outraged and I felt my blood boil.

"Cowards!" I shouted with all my power. "I am your rival , not the girl! You should weigh up with me instead of punishing someone who is innocent and is not to blame."

"Be patient Asteria", I said, "I'm coming."

I untied the goatskin from my hand, put it down and climbed up the osier carefully and by untying and pulling her hair, I managed to free her and bring her down. Such incidents brought me closer to her but I shouldn't forget that she was my permanent test.

I returned to get the goatskin but it wasn't there. It seems that the whole incident was brought about on purpose so that I would have to leave the goatskin with the demons inside and take it away from me. A creepy laughter was heard and smoke filled the entrance.

"Nothing is over yet", the appalling laughter was heard again.

That's too bad, I thought. I've lost my trophy which I was holding with so much pride in order to present it to Mystic Krantor. At least I had the metal which was most important of all. We left the precipice with no more obstacles and arrived at the Temple of Ulios Apollo.

The sun had set and the west was colored in orange and purple. We got in and we needed to wait because Mystic was meditating, as we were told.

We were later noticed and we met him at the statue of the God. He was waiting standing up with a smile on his face and took the pot with the metal from my hands.

"You have an iron will and determination. You can now be called 'iron warrior'", said the Mystic.

We got out and I saw Aetion waiting for us. We took our way back with mixed feelings. I should feel happy that the fifth test was over but I at the same time I felt sorry that Asteria had a bad experience again because of me.

Chapter 24

IN THE EYE OF THE STORM

Two tests remained and I would leave the spirit form and return to the real world. And as the tests became fewer, my anguish for the end became more. Would I make it or would something bad happen and ruin everything at the last moment? And how would I return to reality? What if they were playing a game behind my back and I would stay here eternally!!!!!!!! Questions that remained without answer were torturing me and didn't let me find peace.

What about Asteria? What would happen with her? The truth was that I had got used to her presence because she was associated with so many dangerous, intense and emotionally loaded situations. But what I cared for, was my return and nothing in the world would stop this wish of mine until I achieved it.

Besides, my world was the real one. Not the world of the spirits. I may have been creating stories about Okria on my mind but I didn't want to stay there forever. The days went by full of impatience waiting for Aetion to knock on my door. I jumped up and opened the door for him and he could guess the nervousness that overwhelmed me.

"Yes", I said. "The closer I am to the end of the tests, the more nervous and impatient I become."

We left and as we were getting out, I looked at the blue sphere feeling indecisive. I have done well so far, I thought, let's see what's next. We headed again for the familiar Temple of Apollo Agitor to get Asteria. Aetion left me there and took off as I was waiting for her to show up. When she finally came she wasn't alone. Head Priestess Psamanthi was with her.

"Mystic Ioxos is waiting for you", she said.

"Yes, but aren't we going to a temple", I asked.

"The oracle for the second test", said Psamanthi, "will be given to you here, at the Temple of Agitor by Mystic Ioxos."

Her words seemed weird to me but there wasn't any room for doubts at that point. She took us to the Temple which was now familiar to me and I saw its Mystic for the first time as I hadn't met him before. He was an old man, dressed in gray linen clothes, with a stern face with thin hair and thin white beard.

He looked at me very carefully and I had the same feeling again, that I couldn't hide anything from him. It was as if he was reading my mind when he looked at me. When he finished examining me, he closed his eyes and for a moment I thought that he had fallen asleep. Then he opened them and said, addressing to me, "don't worry. What has been decided will happen, with your participation of course. You have will and faith in what you wish and you will be rewarded." I breathed in and out to send the stress away.

"And now the oracle", I heard Mystic Ioxos saying.

"Seven drops from the metal's vein on the top of Okria", and he showed the familiar pot, at the feet of the Apollo's statue, which was made of Jasper (an opaque rock of virtually any color stemming from the mineral content of the original sediments or ash).

I took it and we left. How is it possible, I thought, for the tin metal to be in a form of drops since it is solid? That oracle was very weird and I couldn't understand it. We got out, passed by Okria, and headed for the top of the mountain.

We first saw pine trees and then cypresses. The path passed through a forest and as we were going up the trees were becoming fewer. We arrived at a glade where what impressed me was the host of broken ceramics there. On some of these pieces, I noticed a few seals. Others had the shape of a flower, others of a cart wheel, others of just a fingerprint and others had two letters written: BA.

I stopped and examined the area and understood that it was an old abandoned forge for ceramics that produced roof tiles. I subconsciously took three pieces of those which had seals on. I did just because I didn't want to forget my love for archaeology. But now at that period being involved in my hobby was a luxury for me. But it's the habit, you see.

I kept the ceramic pieces and we went forward. The path became uphill and there were huge rocks on our left and right. Asteria was walking fast in her familiar way, and I didn't miss a chance to explore the place, as usual, staying behind many times.

We turned right and before us appeared a natural gate like an arch; made of rocks through which there was a path. Out of this natural entrance I discerned a warrior wearing all its equipment. We went near and Asteria, like me, stopped in front of the guard of the gate. I greeted him and I moved forward to enter the gate but he blocked my way.

"You can't go in", he said.

I replied, "you know, I'm on a mission."

"You will enter only if you tell me the names of the maiden Priestesses who were slaughtered by the pirates", he replied.

"But I don't know them", I said.

"I will tell them to you twice", he said slowly, "but you will have to choose the time you will hear them and you will tell them in exactly the same order. If you aren't able to say them even after the second time, you will have to wait for as many years as the names of the maiden Priestesses are in order to be able to come to that gate again."

What can I do, I thought. If that's how it should be done, let it be.

"Are you ready", I heard him saying.

"Yes", I answered and waited.

He took out a scroll on which the names were obviously written, and he began:

AMARYLLIS, ANAKTORIA, ANEMORIA, ANTHILIA, ANTHRAKIA, ARISTARCHI, ARTEMISIA, APHRO, ASTERIA, ATTAVIRIA.

CALLIOPI, CALLISTO, CAPHIRIA, CARPO, CHELIDONIA, CHTONIA, CHRYSOTHOI, CLITIA, CORALLIS, CRINIDA, CRONIA, CRYSTALLIA, CYDONIA.

DELPHOUSIA, DIMOPHILI, DIOMIDIA, DIONI, DORIS, DRYAS.

EFPLIA, EFTHIMIA, EKATI, ERATO,ERISTHENIA, ERIOPI, ESPERIA,

EVARETI,EVDEMONIA, EVDOXIA, EFTERPI, EVRIALI.

GALATI, GLAFKI, GORGINIA, GIRTONI.

IYERIA, IGITORIA, IRIGONI, IFESTIA, IANIRA, IERA, IPPOLITI, IO, IETIS, IMNIA, IPSIPILI.

LAGINIA, LAMPIRIS, LEONTIAS, LEFKOTHEA.

MAKARIA, MEGAKLIA, MELANIA, MELIA, MELITI, MELPOMENI, METAPONTIS, MIRMIDONIA.

NAIAS, NANNO, NIRIIS.

OINO, ORSIIS, OURANIA, OKALIA, ORIA.

PAMPHILI, PARTHENIA, PELAGIA, PHTHIA, PHILOMILA, POLIXO, POLYKRATIA, PSAMANTHI.

RAMANTHIA, RODI, RITIA.

STILVI, STISICHORI, STRATONIKI.

TAYGETI, TEFTLOUSA, TERPSIKRATI, THALIA, THALO, THARGILIA, THELXINIA, THELXINONI.

VALANIA, VEVRIKI, VINASSOS.

XANTHIPI, XANTHO.

ZEFXIPI, ZIRIA, ZIGIA.

Before he finished, I was flabbergasted by the number of the maidens. I could never be able to learn their names, even after the second time he said them. I noticed that he said them in alphabetical order. How many names where they?

The guard, as if he had guessed my curiosity, when he finished, he mentioned that the maiden Priestesses were 12 from each Temple of Apollo. So, I thought that since they were twelve Priestesses and the Temples were nine, we had a hundred and eight Priestesses altogether.

I was desperate. I couldn't think logically with this data. Did that mean that I would have to stay and wait for hundred and eight years before I come again to that gate? It wasn't fair. I sat on a stone making macabre thoughts. I had gone through so many tests, so many obstacles that required boldness, persistence, patience, will and cleverness and I would get stuck because of something so unfair!

Absolutely no one would be able to memorize and say in alphabetical order a hundred and eight names. However hard I tried to think logically, I couldn't find a solution. I stood up in despair, and threw down the ceramic pieces I was holding. That movement woke up something inside me and I addressed to the guard again.

I asked, "So, can you say each name to me slowly?"

"When I told you that you will decide the time you want to hear them, that's what I meant", was the answer.

"So, if a long time intervenes between the names is it alright?" I asked.

"No, it's your decision. We can start in the morning and finish at night", he said.

That was it. I had found the solution.

"Stay here", I said to Asteria, "and I'll be there in minute."

I left running back to the path, until I reached the old forge for ceramics. I picked up as many pieces as I could hold in my hands and returned. I did the same route twice estimating they will be enough.

Then I searched and found a small sharp stone, sat down, spread the ceramic pieces and told the guard to start with the first name. When I finished carving on the ceramic, I told him to say the second and I went on by putting numbers in front of them so that I wouldn't confuse the alphabetical order. The only problem I was facing was the exhaustion in my fingers because I had to press hard in order to carve so many names on the ceramics.

But, I had found the way to memorize the names, although it seemed an insurmountable obstacle in the beginning. It was morning when we went to Okria's gate and the sun was beginning to set while

I was writing the last names. When I finished with all of them, I started reading them to the guard and after that he asked me to perform libation for the maiden Priestesses. I had no idea but Asteria helped me with that.

"The gate is open now", said the guard and disappeared.

Without wasting any more time I went in and we moved along the path. As we were walking, we met goats and sheep which were running to get out of the gate descending the top. But that wouldn't impress me so much if I didn't see other animals going down in a hurry. Snakes, tortoises, lizards, mice, birds, even snails which usually hibernate during the winter underground waiting to feel the first rain to wake up. They had broken their protective cover in order to escape from the top as fast as possible.

Something scary, something that frightened them, was coming and they had sensed the danger and ran in a panic to save themselves. There's no other explanation. We were the only ones going towards the opposite direction. All creatures were running away scared.

I felt a shiver throughout my body for the unknown. What would that be? We moved forward a bit more reaching almost the top, when a hellish wind started blowing, uprooting everything. Were holding on the rocks and crawling on our hands and knees as we couldn't walk normally because we would fall down.

As the time passed, the wind became stronger and it was obvious that the only thing we could do was hang on to the rocks without moving. A whirlwind was spinning on the top and black clouds appeared rotating with the wind. The scenery was nightmarish that frightened you only at the sight of it.

A figure began shaping at the centre of the whirlwind and it stabilized at the top. A huge supernatural man wearing a black tunic with his hands raised giving the impression that this scary scenery was created by the energy of his fingertips. The wind was spinning around him and the clouds above him were nearly touching him. Nature was obeying his will. Then a voice was heard as if it was coming from an underground tunnel, which gave the creeps.

"You stupid, weak creatures, look and feel Nohra's power", said the voice. "I am the wind that lifts the ground and turns it upside down. That makes the clouds run away. That gives power to the storms and makes high waves in the sea. I am the heart and the soul of the one who spins the wind; showing my power to Earth and making people shiver from fear and hide.

I inflate the sails of the boats for centuries now, and smash the trees that resist me. I run throughout the

Earth to bring the new, the change. I am the breath of the Earth, its life. I loathe the silence and the rut, I am disgusted by serenity and deadlock. These words are only for the dead. Creation needs action, motion like the Earth, like the planets, like the Universe. What stands still is dead."

There was thick darkness everywhere and a storm was about to break out. Then Nohra's voice was heard again. He still had his hands raised as if he was conducting this appalling orchestra of nature's elements which were ready to start their gruesome, merciless concert.

"I'm calling the primal elements of Aloades, demon Aktorion, who is the flash of lightning and demon Molion, who is the power of thunder. They were born in the darkness of creation and since their birth they are in a constant war with Apollo and I am calling them in order to show their power to that weak doormat who had the impertinence to raise his eyes from the ground", said Nohra.

A sharp voice was heard saying:

> "I turn the day into night and my rage bursts against anyone who dares to raise his eyes from the ground, anything that takes pride in its height, inanimate or alive. People, trees, houses, mountain tops have tried and still try my power. I can smash stone and metals and burn whatever I touch. No one can compete with me."

After Aktorion, the thunderous voice of Molion was heard:

> "I am the thunder and I make every human creature shiver at my hearing and hide into the holes of the Earth. My power is such that can make the Earth shake as if there is earthquake and everything becomes silent at my hearing.
>
> My din brings about landfall and together with my brother Aktorion we are a death weapon. So where do you think you are going, you weak frightened little person? With whom are you going to compete? Don't you know that this top belongs to us? Go back. Hide in the ground. Save yourself. Apollo can't help you, even if you invoke him."

I was shaking with fear and when I heard the first thunder I almost lost my voice and my hearing. It struck near me, breaking the rocks and the flash of lightning blinded me. Now I had to search for a place to protect ourselves, not for the metal. The lightning went on making the Earth shake and smashing the rocks. I found a rock for protection and what impressed me was that the lightning was striking at a specific part of the rocks which was catching fire and giving off smoke.

I thought of something but couldn't dare to find out whether it was really happening. I thought that, because the metals attract lightning, maybe the metal was there! I had to try and find out, though it was too risky to be near the lightning. But I had to see if my thought was right.

I moved along carefully, after saying to Asteria to stay behind the rock, and by making small steps I went as near as I could. Thunder clapped and its lightning blinded me while my ears were hurting by its power. However, I tried to keep my eyes open so that I could see the spot where it was striking.

So I saw the metal shining. It had nearly melted by the constant lightning and it was dissolving into the ground. I couldn't do anything. I didn't have that power. The metal was melting and disappearing and I realized that my thought was correct.

No matter how hard I tried to find a solution to get some of the metal, I couldn't. Only if the lightning stopped could it be possible. But the lightning went on and the metal was melting. I returned disappointed to Asteria and explained to her what was happening.

"Too bad", I said. "This must be the end. I will return with bare hands and I will remain a spirit in Okria for ever."

I wanted to cry, shout, swear for everything that was going to waste in such an unfair way together with my future. I was outraged and as I was going out of the rock that protected us I shouted angrily, "hit me. Hit here, and I showed them my chest."

I felt a hand pulling me backwards and I fell on my back. I made it at the last minute. The next minute the lightning hit where I had sat before, creating a big crater. I looked at Asteria who made that life-saving movement, otherwise I would be coal now by the lightning's fire.

"Thank you", I said, but it was pointless anymore. I wanted to go back. Now that this couldn't happen, I didn't care to live in that form. A tear rolled on my cheek, expressing the bitterness I felt.

The lightning went on but the storm inside me was stronger than that outside. I glanced at the metal's vein for the last time but it had disappeared. It was lost for ever. I had two more days to try but since I wouldn't be able to get the metal, time meant nothing to me. I left with a heavy heart, while there was a chaos behind me. Nohra had won!!!

I was descending in a really bad mood, dragging because of my disappointment, when I heard strange songs and voices coming from the slot on a rock, if I understood correctly. I stopped to listen. Indeed, the voices were coming from there. I went near carefully and ducked to see but I couldn't see well. I went more inside being careful with my steps and, to my surprise, I saw a cave where the small Silini were singing and transferring something into small stone cups.

I went even more down to see better with Asteria behind me, but I accidentally bumped a stone with my foot and they suddenly stopped and turned to my side. But I managed to see that they were collecting something that was dripping, something shiny from a part of the underground cave.

"You know", I spoke first, "your song came to my ears and I got in to listen to it better."

Though they didn't seem hostile, they were still annoyed, as I could see from their look.

One said to me, "stranger, why are you interrupting us? We have no time to waste. You came during our most sacred moment which happens every 100 years, when we collect the valuable tin metal. it took us 100 years of praying to make it happen and now you've come to spoil our celebration?"

"I'm sorry", I said. I didn't want to be the reason for this to happen and a flame of hope sparkled inside me. Maybe nothing is really lost after all.

"Go away as fast as you can", they said.

"It's a matter of life and death", I pleaded, "and I would like to ask you to give me a few drops of the metal if it is possible."

They laughed and said, "we are not giving away this metal."

"But I'm asking only a few drops. It's a matter of life and death", I repeated, while cold sweat was rolling on my forehead.

This was my last chance and I was determined to do anything to persuade them to, whatever the cost was. They gathered forming a circle and started conferring for a long time and my suspense was at the top about what decision they would make.

After much time, one of them said, "we will give you less than nine drops and more than five if you answer correctly to three puzzles."

I had no other choice so I nodded my head while Asteria was watching standing at the entrance behind me.

"First puzzle", said one Silinos. "What makes our life better but we can't hold in our hands".

A thousands thoughts crossed my mind but under the stress and the agony to complete the task having only one chance, I had a block. No logical answer came to my mind. No, I thought. You have to think. You have to put logic before feelings.

There was silence. Everyone was waiting for my answer while I was thinking. If I answered 'wind', we can't hold it but it doesn't improve our life either. It is our life. Because without oxygen, we can't breathe and so we wouldn't exist. Water, on the other hand, helps our life but we can hold it. So what's left? Fire. Fire had all the features. It has improved our life since its discovery but we can't hold it.

"Fire", I said flatly having doubts about the result.

Praising voices were heard and Silinos said, "you have three drops of the metal."

"Second puzzle", said another, "what enters everywhere without asking?"

I was encouraged by the first right answer and was waiting for the second one calmly even though it seemed ambiguous or having more than one answer. In a room enters the noise, the smoke, the dust, the sun, the latest on certain conditions. The dust and the smoke enter because the air transfers them. So there are two left. The sound and the wind.

"I have two answers", I said. "The one is the wind and the other is the sun."

"You have answered correctly", said one. "We had the wind in mind but the sound, now that you are saying it, may be accepted as a right answer."

Praising voices again and Silinos said, "you have two more drops of the metal."

"The third and last puzzle", someone else said. "It fertilizes the Earth."

That seemed easy and there was no other answer but the water. Besides, I thought a bit cleverly. First was fire, then wind so water was left.

"The water", I said and there was praising again.

"You have won fairly seven drops of the metal", said one. "And you know, it isn't a simple metal. it has got other qualities because it has been struck by thunder on the top of Okria."

He counted seven Silini, who had come where I was, holding the stone cups. In each one there was one drop of the metal and they put in my palms seven drops of the metal which were now cold and solid. The last one gave me the stone cup together with the drop.

"I can't thank you enough", I said. "If it hadn't been for you, I wouldn't have been able to get the metal."

"Remember", said one. "You haven't seen us, you haven't met us and if they ask you tell them that they are wrong."

"I give you my word, it isn't going to happen from my part", I said.

I stood up and left through the entrance of the cave jumping with joy. I proceeded and then I thought that the stone metal was useless for me because I had put the drops in the pot from the Temple. So I returned to give them back the stone metal because I didn't need it.

But I was surprised to discover that there was nothing but rocks at the place where the cave's entrance was. It can't have been my imagination, I said, and I quickly saw into the pot made of jasper to check if the metal was still there.

They were still there. The stone cup, too. I had no logical explanation for this. Neither had Asteria who made an enigmatic grimace when I asked her. Full of questions we made our way back thinking of what had happened. If it hadn't been for Asteria, not only would the test fail, but I also wouldn't exist anymore because of my thoughtless act of provoking the power of lightning.

With no more hitches, we returned to the Temple of Agitoras Apollo, where Ioxos was waiting for us. Full of joy, which was obvious on my face, I gave him the pot. He was looking at me with a smile.

"You are one step before the end", he said, "and your faith brings you always back to the Temple as a winner. So you can now be called 'vanquisher of the demons'."

I was really proud and happy and I saw Asteria who was watching the conversation calm and inexpressive. Still, she helped me carry out my task again today. Without her I would be in the ashes now.

I returned together with Aetion with feeling of joy overwhelming me. I was close to achieving my goal and I had every reason to be happy about it. But I wasn't done yet. One test was left and I would be free of the bondage that kept me in Okria. I shouldn't allow myself to get carried away.I could do that after the completion of the final test.

CHAPTER 25

THE GATE OF THE UNDERWORLD

So I had reached my final test; having overcome many obstacles and having felt many thrills, disappointments and joy and having got to know a strange world, not exactly as I had imagined and created it in my fantasy. As I looked at it in my imagination from a distance, I could see only its positive side. I hadn't entered it to experience and understand how difficult it was to survive through all the dangers lurking every moment and having to fight with Nohra's demons every day.

As Aetion had told me, the fighting was on a daily basis in all levels, with an enemy that used whatever means to annihilate and eliminate them. How long had I been there? I didn't know. I had lost the track of time.

I looked at the blue sphere that was floating at the corner. I had never taken it with me neither did I intend to do so. I didn't need more worries and trouble in my head. Power is something you should know well before using it. Otherwise, it leads you to uncontrollable paths, it makes you its slave even when you think you can control it.

What has gotten into me now, making me philosophize? I was probably doing it so as not to think my final challenge on which depended my return to the real world. As much as I was trying to avoid it, it was beyond my power. I had to go through the seventh test so that what I wanted so much wouldn't remain just a dream.

I drained my memory like a sponge, bringing back to it every single thing of my life which I hadn't recalled before. My father, my mother and my childhood came back to my memory and all the hardship I had gone through on the island and in Athens. A life of eighteen years plus, which matured me abruptly.

The other children at my age didn't have other worries except for how to spend their parents' pocket money and with which girl they will go out. The night school, the grind and the negative aspect of my staying in Athens were brought back to my memory.

That got me to my childhood. There at the lonely rock of Marathounda beach where I was sitting next to Astradeni, who was trying to catch my eye and get me into playing a game she wanted. I was engrossed in my thoughts and fiction that I didn't pay much attention to her though she always involved me in her games. I wonder where she is.

And what a strange name she has, which you hear only on Symi; Astradeni. What's its derivation? Astradeni Astra-deni (astra=stars, deni=ties. The girl that ties the stars). She must be a big girl now, about seventeen years old, and I won't recognize her if I ever come across her. Maybe she doesn't live on the island anymore. I would have known it.

My seventh trial came to my mind again. The last one, which was full of symbolism because of the number seven, but also because gold metal is a connective part on the Okria symbol. As much as I don't want to admit it, there are symbols and symbolisms everywhere. Some of them are evident and some not.

The numbers, the letters, and the shapes have their own secret language when they are placed in a certain way, when they are pronounced and written on selected places and acquire, because of time, space and special ceremonies, another potential, dimension and energy. I have become aware of that a great deal during my stay in Okria. Everything happens for a reason. Everything has got an explanation and special relation.

But let's return to more practical and interesting things. The oracle would probably be given to me by Mystic Hyperinor, since he represented the gold metal. So I would go to the Temple of Miragetis

Apollo where I had seen, with the help of the Mystic, the secret world of the spirits and creatures.

I felt a pain in my stomach remembering all these frightening creatures, some of which I had already come across during my tests. And while my mind was 'travelling' I heard knockings on the door. It was Aetion who announced me that we would go to the Temple of Agitor Apollo.

"Why?" I asked.

"Because today they celebrate 'Agitoria', when the small statue of the god is transferred from a secret crypt - which only Priests, Priestesses and Mystics know, and it is forbidden for everyone else to see it - and they perform a procession of the statue around the Temple, chanting hymns", said Aetion.

This celebration takes place annually to honor god Apollo and in memory of the incident that brought the Dorians to these places. In the old days, he went on talking, the statue used to be transferred to all the nine Temples and then it was returned to the secret crypt. But because of the fact that this was tiring and the older people couldn't follow, it takes place now only in the Temple of Agitor, where the statue is.

With our discussion we arrived at the Temple, where there were many people in order to watch the ceremony, formally dressed and some children were wearing palm tree leaves which was one of the god's symbols. A bell was heard and the voices stopped, while a hymn was heard from inside the Temple which was getting louder. Then, a group of Priestesses appeared at the entrance which were chanting in pairs.

Behind that group, some Priests were holding the statue of the god, behind them was Mystic Ioxos and after him a second group of Priestesses completed the procession. The people bowed before the statue which they processed once around the Temple and then they stopped there was absolute silence and Mystic Ioxos was heard saying, "come Priestesses of Phoebus. Chant for the god with the golden hair so that he lives eternally in his nine homes on Symi and protect the island from the evil."

The Priestesses started chanting again as the process proceeded again for another turn. I discerned Asteria among the Priestesses dressed in different clothes, formal ones for this special occasion, laurel-crowned. She was very beautiful.

After the third procession, the faithful ran to touch the statue in order to get strength and the procession went inside the Temple and the Priestesses appeared again holding sweets made of wheat, honey and nuts to give them to the people for blessing. Asteria saw me and came to me with a smile on her face and I took a sweet she offered me. I thanked her and she left in a hurry.

"That was all", said Aetion. "We are going back."

On our way back, people who were returning from the celebration, were passing near us. What worried me was that they were treating me as if I were a member of the Okria society. Would I never leave? Is that why they considered me one of them? I was really troubled when I made those thoughts and I should really be worried.

CHAPTER 26

The time went by and the big moment arrived. It was the final countdown for a positive or negative result. I didn't want to think about the second possibility even though it was likely to happen and I would stay a spirit in Okria forever or even worse I would end up in Chaos.

If I should remain a spirit in Okria, I would rather not exist. I'd rather disappear in Chaos instead of dying every day. I was so stressed, that I was pacing without being able to stand still for more than a few minutes. Instead of waiting for a knocking on the door I kept opening it to see if Aetion was coming, even though that was a risk with all I had been through from Nohra. When he finally came, he announced me something different from what I was expecting.

"At the oracle of Apollo?" I asked him, repeating what I had heard.

"Yes", said Aetion.

"But aren't we going to the Temple of Miragetis Apollo where Hyperinor is?" I said.

He replied, "that's what they told me so that's what I'm telling you."

"Has anything changed?" I asked in agony and my doubts and queries for my future which seemed blurry and uncertain.

Aetion didn't answer. All my trying has gone to waste? I didn't know what to assume. Unfortunately, it wasn't up to me to influence or change the situation. Whichever Okria's choice was, I had to obey.

But why did I have to accept what they told me without protesting? I will protest for the injustice and the breaking of the agreements we had made. Oh God! What was I saying? I wasn't myself because of the psychological pressure I was under.

But why had I prejudged my future without seeing the final outcome and the reason of my visit at Apollo's oracle? I should keep calm, I thought to myself. Just let it be. It's better for me to be calm and sensible -as much as this was possible- rather than nervous and worried taking the risk of making mistakes because I was emotionally overloaded.

"Let's go", I said to Aetion decisively, and we set off.

We got out of Okria's settlement and headed for the Temple of Agitoras Apollo,as far as I understood. So, we were going to get Asteria. Indeed, we arrived at the Temple where she was waiting for us. We took her with us, and, by changing direction, we went west and got into a forest with cypresses.

After covering much distance, we arrived at the old castle. We passed it by and about 100 meters after it, Aetion put aside a few 'skina' and discovered an opening in which many steps appeared to be leading to the core of the Earth. Aetion said goodbye to us there and left.

I remained outside the entrance, indecisive and Asteria was next me. But why was I waiting? Would someone come to invite me in? I had to make the start. I decided to go down and nodded Asteria to follow me.

We descended more than twenty steps and arrived at a corridor, at the end of which there was a door made of iron and out of it there was a person dressed in white, holding a small crater and a cup and seemed to be a Priest.

"You are at the Oracle of Apollo in Kapsos and according to the ritual of the oracle you will have to drink from this drink - he showed us the crater - in order for you to be allowed to enter the interior", said the Priest.

We couldn't do anything else, since it was obligatory .We will go through it too. I went to get the cup of his hands which he had filed with the drink of the crater. It had a bitter taste and at the same time a sweet taste with an aroma of various herbs. When I had drank it all, I felt a sweet exhaustion on my limbs.

I moved forward without realizing it towards the door which had opened. I got in and I was in Varouha. But how is this possible? I thought. I got into from the door and I am in Varouha? Unbelievable!

But what was even more unbelievable, was that at the Varouha valley there were armies ready to fight. From one side, there was the Okria's army armed having as leaders the heroes wearing shiny uniforms and armors, each one representing different kinds of armaments. Cavalrymen, javelin throwers, lancers, archers, soldiers holding spears in various sizes, double axes, hooks and other strange weapons.

On the other side, were the demons of Nohra and all the other evils that ally with him, shouting with hatred and a feeling of revenge waving their guns. With rhythmic screams and knocking the ground they were causing pandemonium in order to scare those opposite them.

As I was watching the army of Okria, I discerned Aetion who was the leader of the lancers. As soon as he saw me, he called me to go near him. I went and looked closely at the armors and weapons in admiration while the flags and standards with Okria's symbol on, were waving high in the sky.

"Will you put up with all of them?" I asked Aetion feeling awe.

Aetion said, "it's not the first time."

"Who are all these next to Nohra?" I asked as I was looking at their weird uniforms and their strange weapons feeling terrified by their voices and shouting but more by their appalling face which was animal-like and monstrous.

Aetion replied, "let's start from the left. These are Gliodes Marmaristes, then Green and Black Minigi, Varvi, Trimurii, Vrayes, Drimonii, Zagrites Thirephtes, Thrapsii Vrahistes, Chrantores Bladehands, Vrvouhii Sharpteeth, Multitentacled Phates, Melanes Karii, Feathered Porkis, Fastfeet Mazdeki, One-eyed Chaleggi, Triovolistes Grenii, Unicorned Martigges, Survii Sculpbreakers, Gergeni Shaggy, Oxblood Dolites, Thoumi, Pihti and Lorygges. Behind them we the big monsters could be discerned. Poliakantha, Flyki, Targones, Tharki, Klites and Armia.

"Will you fight with all of them?" I asked Aetion in fright again, not being able to believe that Aetion had given me a positive answer before.

"Of course", he replied.

"But they are a hundred times bigger than you. You don't stand a chance", I said.

"Now, turn around and look behind you", he said.

I looked behind Okria's army and I was agape. The Mystics were ten times bigger, formally dressed with a floating sphere above each one's head, like the one Hyperinor had given me but this one was purple and much bigger in size. They were holding Okria's symbol on one hand and on the other a sword which wasn't solid but airy in deep blue color. I gulped feeling impressed by the scenery.

"Come and get your position because the battle is about to begin", I heard Aetion saying.

"Are you talking to me?" I asked. "But I don't belong here."

To which Aetion replied, "you belong here. Look at the weapon that is waiting for you!"

I looked at where he was pointing and indeed, I saw a sling on the ground.

"No, I don't belong here", I shouted. "I don't belong here. I don't belong here."

The pitch of my voice was so high that my throat was sore and I opened my eyes. I was at the point where we had passed by the door of the Oracle and Asteria was next to me waiting patiently.

"Have I left this place?" I asked her in a low voice.

No, she answered with a nod.

"Was it an illusion?" I asked.

Yes, she answered with a nod again.

Then I asked, "have you left at all?"

No.

What did all that I had seen mean? Was there an explanation or was I under the influence of the drink I had had? But I had also forgotten the reason why I was there. Why was I here, really? I looked around and discovered that I wasn't alone. I was in a round chamber and eyes behind masks were looking at me. The atmosphere was suffocating because of the smoke.

"Where am I?" I asked, feeling scared.

"At the Oracle of Apollo", answered the one sitting at the centre, and behind him the rest of them were lining up in dyads, triads, groups of four, five, six and seven, dressed in the same way.

Then I said, "why am I here?"

"To learn the oracle for the seventh challenge," was the reply.

There was an awkward silence omnipresent, and suddenly the same voice was heard behind a mask which belonged to the one who was respected and obeyed by everyone in a hierarchy.

"God Apollo, the God of light, music, soothsaying, medicine, order and the harmony of the universe will guide you like the bellwether that leads the flock of sheep. What you saw before are real. You have just been to the future sooner, to a fight that will take place soon", said a familiar voice.

"Whatever the outcome of the seventh challenge is", he spoke again, "you are already a winner. If you fail, you will stay in Okria with us and the position you saw belongs to you. If you pass the test, you will return to your world."

Then the voice said, "I invited you into this sacred place of Apollo on purpose. You have already learned so many secrets that we consider you one of us. You have fought Nohra and managed to overcome all obstacles. So, it is now time for the seventh oracle of the seventh test to be announced to you. Are you ready?"

"Yes", I replied.

"At Varouha, into the Earth's depths, three entrances, two exits, one labyrinth, one choice. At the chamber of water, the metal inside the metal", he said and then there was silence.

After a while, he was heard again saying, "you will find the place at Varouha on your own."

I heard it all and was puzzled and confused at both the oracle and everything that strange guy said. And even though I thought that the procedure of hearing the oracle was over, I remembered the sacred pot which I normally should have been given in the Temple so that I would put the metal inside. But that moment something weird and amazing happened.

The lines that had been formed by the guys that looked the same began uniting with the first until they all became one. First the group of seven, then the six then the five, the four, the three, the two. They all merged into the first one at the center who said to me, as if he had read my mind.

"Come and get the pot made of Agate", and as soon as he took the mask off, I recognized Mystic Hyperinor.

So he was the rest of the men. They were aspects of himself. But how could they function separately? That is a mystery, I thought. I went very enthusiastically and in admiration and took the pot from his hands. I felt awe and embarrassment before him, like I felt on the first day of school.

He was so strong that the distance between it and my weakness seemed like abyss. I also believed that for as long as Hyperinor existed, I could feel more secure that justice would prevail. But could anything be sure in the world of spirits? I don't know.

We left the Oracle of Apollo and headed for Varouha passing through Okria. Now, I would have to find the entrances of the cave on my own, without Asteria's help. Who would be the best to tell me that? The shepherds and farmers of the area of course, I thought. As soon as e got there, we met a shepherd with his animals at the valley.

"Hello", I greeted him.

He greeted me back.

"Can I ask you something?" I said.

He seemed willing to answer me.

"Is there a cave at Varouha?" I asked.

"Yes", he replied.

Next I asked, "do you know where its entrance is?"

"On the east there is an entrance but I would advise you not to go there", he said.

"Why?" I asked.

"Because you will get lost. There is a labyrinth in there which we don't know where it ends", he said.

Here we are, I thought when I heard about the labyrinth. I thanked him and we headed east but however hard I tried I didn't manage to track the entrance. That moment, I saw someone on a mule.

"Do you know the opening of the cave that is here?" I asked him after greeting him.

"It is behind that big oak-tree that is taller than all the other trees", he said, "but I don't believe that you want to go there."

"Why?" I asked.

"Because it is a deep precipice", he replied.

"Do you mean that there isn't a cave underneath?" I asked.

"No one goes there easily because it is dangerous", was the answer.

Once again I asked, "why?"

"Besides the fact that it is difficult to descend because you need a rope, there are dangerous demons and creatures there", he replied.

I thanked him and headed for the big oak tree. As soon as I got there, I moved forward and saw the opening. It was indeed a precipice which you couldn't descent. I took a stone and threw it and for a long time we could hear the noise it was making as it was rolling and hitting on the walls of the precipice. I had to forget about that entrance. Nothing could be done from here.

We left heading west of the Varouha valley and where the rocks began, we could see an entrance. We went near, but it was just a small cave that could room only four or five people. I was disappointed because I was wasting my time without result. We headed south and at the center we found some farmers drawing water from a well.

"Hello", I greeted them. "Do you happen to know a cave here at Varouha?"

"There were many", said one of them. "That one is difficult and dangerous."

"Never mind, I have decided to go", I replied.

"The entrance is north, where the valley ends, in a cluster of rocks that look like human figures from far - they say that they are people who turned to stones because of their fear. But if you want my advice, don't go. We don't pass even outside of that place", said one.

"Why?" I asked.

"Because, it is haunted by evil powers and it is a labyrinth inside. Whoever got into there never returned", was the reply.

I shivered from fear and shuddered at the hearing of all this.

They went on to say, "it is said that screams are heard from inside, said the second farmer, and that strange things happen even in front of the entrance. That's why we never go near there. It is the gate of the Underworld."

Oh God, where was I going, I thought. They all describe it to me so dramatically. But there was another entrance, since we have already found the other two. It was probably on the west where we had come from. Maybe that was the best one.

We went back searching, but in vain. I couldn't decide which entrance to enter from. There was no way I would enter the precipice, the other one was presented as the gate of the Underworld, so I had to find a third one and give it a try. That moment, three people were coming up to the valley. I greeted them and asked them if there was a cave west of Varouha.

"No", they said all at the same time. But they all knew the opening on the North that the other two had also told me but said we shouldn't try to enter it because we wouldn't get out from there alive and it would be so sad because we were too young to die.

Finally, there was no other entrance than the one on the north which nobody wanted to pass even out of it. Unfortunately I had to try from there. I took all the courage I had with me and set off feeling numb. It would be the final trial and the hardest of all as it seemed according to what everybody said.

We reached the north part of the valley of Varouha and a strange silence was omnipresent. We found the human figures easily, the opening of the cave was under them. I stood hesitantly before the entrance afraid of what I had been told and didn't dare to make the step. But without entering and getting the gold medal, I wouldn't be able to return to the real world that I wanted so much. I had no other choice, it was a one-way decision and a matter of courage.

Out of my fear for everything that I would encounter and even the probability of failure, I couldn't move my feet. I stood still looking at the opening as if I were hypnotized. Also, I wouldn't have any help from anywhere so the outcome depended on my power and trying. I took a deep breath as if I would dive and gestured Asteria to move forward.

We got in and what welcomed us was the silence and the humidity. My ears and all parts of my body were alert, waiting for a move, a reaction. From where? From anywhere. The opening was big and deep going left and forming a chamber. In the chamber there were stalagmites and there was fog, maybe because of humidity.

We moved through the fog and I felt I was suffocating. As if I had run out of oxygen. The same was happening to Asteria. There was something going wrong but I didn't know what it was. Suddenly, the fog started moving, shaping and re-shaping. It took several shapes and figures and at the same time, voices and shouts of bodiless creatures were heard, becoming louder each time.

What felt like fog in the chamber had nothing to do with humidity after all. It was probably bodiless creatures that were in the room and we had activated them with our passing by. There was a fight with the demons who wanted to keep us there and not let us proceed. The demons were surrounding us and we couldn't move on. It was as if we had stuck in a kind of invisible glue which didn't let us move. When we unstuck one foot the other one got stuck as well as our hands. It would be a mistake to go back. We had to move on with all the power we had, making our way in great difficulty. That's what we did.

The good thing was that the further we were moving from the chamber, the weaker the bodiless demons were becoming. That chamber should be their residence. We were breathing heavily as if we were running in a marathon because we were trying to escape from that living fog in which we had gotten stuck.

We arrived at the end of the chamber really exhausted. We lied down weak and heavy like bags in order to have some rest. The fog was gathering behind us, condensing and changing shapes. In the end it took the shape of a snake and went away. I was relieved because we wouldn't face it again.

The delay in finding the opening of the gate for the seventh test had wasted our time and the sun was about to set. We were at the point where we had two options. Two openings. Which one should we follow?

I followed the one on the right but that got us into a complicated tunnel where we couldn't find the beginning nor the end of it. I needed to get out of the labyrinth, as the oracle said, and go back to follow the other entrance.

Desperate and exhausted, we were wandering around the same places without hope. I couldn't find a solution. I was in despair. Asteria was suffering with me throughout this hardship, following my choices. I couldn't continue. I made an attempt to get out of the labyrinth and go back but got into a narrow and long chamber and on its walls I could discern some patterns which were not very clear. I went nearer and discovered that they were prehistoric animals and figures being drawn by people of the Paleolithic era. Probably that part had been inhabited by people many years ago.

I was so tired that I couldn't take it anymore. I let myself fall down, as my eyes were closing because I hadn't slept well the previous night waiting for the seventh test to begin and because of today's searching. But even though I closed my eyes I didn't let myself relax nor surrender to Morpheus (the god of sleep). The fear that something unexpected might happen kept me alert. But on the other hand I felt sleepy.

I was opening and closing my eyes and suddenly I heard a noise from the ground. As if something was moving underground. The noises multiplied and suddenly human bones appeared near me. I stressed and stuck on the wall so as not to come into contact with them. But they kept coming out forming two human skeletons. After they had been completed, they stayed up shaking as if they were afraid of something.

There was a new sound and other human bones started coming up and assembling. On the right and left side of the chamber the skeletons that must have been buried during the prehistoric time couldn't stay underground. They wanted to get out. Something terrible and unknown was coming from the ground that made them wake up from the eternal sleep and want to escape.

The whole corridor was filled with skeletons from the left and right and the sound of the bones crashing against each other created a macabre music that I couldn't bear. If that kept longer, it would drive me mad. In the meantime, I saw something that I couldn't believe my eyes.

The drawings of the animals and people on the rocks, started moving, slowly in the beginning, and then became more intense. It was a schizophrenic, mad scenery for which there was no logical explanation. A loud noise was heard from the earth that seemed like an earthquake and the skeletons trembled more, bringing about a creepy concert with the crashing of their bones.

The roar was getting more intense and I was sure that something terrible was about emerge from the depths of the Earth. I called Asteria so that we could both leave but it was too late. The skeletons were shaking with fear and poured out towards the exit and as a result we bumped into them bringing about a pandemonium.

We were on the ground with bones crashing against each other. The roar was even more intense and the ground was cracking. We were tangled up with the skeletons and the only solution was to go towards the direction they were going. We managed to stand up and leave the ground but the skeletons were crashing in their attempt to leave quickly and we were falling down with them.

We were stepping on bones everywhere because many of them had fallen apart. In the meantime, the drawings on the walls had disappeared moving towards the exit; following the skeletons. The chasing lasted a long while and the roar kept following us. It seems that the skeletons that had known the exit for centuries, led us to the right place and we got to the entrance of the cave. We got out and saw the valley of Varouha following the skeletons to escape what was coming from the depths of the earth.

Unfortunately, I wouldn't be able to find the metal this way. But when the skeletons, even the drawings on the walls leave the residence they had been living for centuries, you can't think positively especially with the roaring like an earthquake shaking your feet. It makes you want to run away and save yourself.

To tell the truth though, this exit was a good chance for us to get fresh air after all we had been through in the cave. Just as I was thinking about that, black clouds appeared above the valley. The most amazing thing was that as soon as they were touching the summit of Okria, they turned into huge prehistoric animals which descended towards us. There was no chance you could escape and save yourself.

The skeletons appeared again, those that were left, and were running towards the cave to be saved. I thought we should go there too, but this time following the left entrance after the chamber with the fog. The huge animals were roaring making the earth tremble and were approaching the valley of Okria spreading panic.

A scene from hell, with the skeletons squeezing at the entrance of the cave and outside the danger arriving represented by the heavy big prehistoric animals. Fortunately the opening was too narrow for the animals to fit in and enter. That's why the skeletons had chosen it for their salvation as they had already known that.

We also entered while the huge animals were fighting with each other. The carnivorous were eating the herbivorous ones, and the screams of those that were dying and were hurt echoed from miles away and we were watching this macabre scenery from the safety of the cave's opening. A massacre was taking place before our astonished eyes.

But that spectacle shouldn't delay us. The test was expecting me, as well as the metal, and I had to find a way to continue till the end. We moved on at the left entrance after the chamber where we had seen the fog previously, with all our senses alert.

The deep roar had stopped and there was absolute silence, which I thought wasn't so good because you didn't know what would happen suddenly. We had been walking for a long time in a tunnel with many turns and curves on the ground; others going upwards and others downwards, and at some point we saw light coming from high up.

As soon as I saw it, I became more careful in my walking and was moving with precaution just in case. As we were getting nearer, I discovered that the light was coming from an opening of the precipice which we had visited on its surface and I had thrown the stone to estimate its depth.

The bad thing was that the precipice was cutting the road of the underground tunnel leaving just a narrow passage where we could barely walk. When we went near, we saw that something weird had begun. Various feathered creature from the depths of the earth were going up and down from the precipice leaving fluorescence behind them.

We remained there watching; ecstatic. We finally discovered that the feathered creatures that were running towards the exit of the precipice were being hunted by others which had been decimated and were trying to save themselves. The first creatures were two inches and looked like dragonflies. The other ones behind them were double in size and looked like bats. They attacked the smaller ones, and killed the ones they grabbed by biting them on their neck and then they would fall into the precipice screaming.

We were watching without being able to do anything in that macabre chasing and suddenly one creature that was being run after, came on our side and sat on Asteria's shoulder. The other that was running it after, tried to attack it and it perched nearer too Asteria looking at her in the eyes begging her to help it. It had a human body, very long fingers and toes, slashed eyes, and small feelers on its head.

I didn't think much. I jumped in front of Asteria to protect it. The bat-like creature left and soon a swarm of them came to us to ask for explanations. They tried to scare us by screaming so that we wouldn't defend the weak feathered creature that had stuck on Asteria watching what was happening in fear.

More dark bat-likes arrived and I searched for something that would help me defend myself.

There were stones and a stick that had either fallen or someone else had dropped it and it had stuck on the wall of the precipice. I told Asteria to stand up and follow me until the point where the big branch of the tree was; together with our feathered creature that was under our protection.

So with me at the front and Asteria behind, we walked slowly and reached the branch. I pulled it from the wall and brought it on the ground while the bat-like creatures were flying and growling. I broke two pieces of the branch so that I could use them more efficiently and moved them around my head to try them.

The black flying creatures understood my intentions and started retreating towards the precipice, notifying the others that were hunting the small ones and as a result they quitted the hunting and hid inside the depths of the earth. Then the other small ones gathered around us screaming joyfully doing acrobatics in the air.

It doesn't matter they can't talk like us, I thought. The expression of joy and gratitude doesn't need a language to be said. They are obvious on the faces and movements they were making to thank us. But it was about time our feathered friend returned to its company. He didn't feel like doing it though. It wanted to stay with us more.

How could I explain to it that the place we were going to was even more dangerous? I tried to tell it with words and show it with gestures but without result. I had no other way. It kept flying around us without following the rest. I thought that it would disappear on the first difficulty we encountered.

The others that were like it had left from the opening and were remained looking at the precipice which ended nowhere. We had to go to other side stepping carefully on the only passage on the right of the precipice in order to go on. I started first with my back against the wall and my eyes looking down at the chaos but it was impossible to avoid looking at it. The more I looked at it, the more I felt that something was pulling me downwards and could bare to continue.

I decided to return and start again with my back turned on the precipice and my hands holding the walls for more safety. My legs were shaking and when I got to the middle I was in cold sweat because of my agony and all my trying. The sweat was getting into my eyes, irritating them.

A bit after the middle of the route, I didn't step carefully and I stumbled but I managed to hold on with my hands. I stood still to gain my confidence back and recover so that I could reach the end, having been all sweaty because of the humidity in the atmosphere. Now I was on the other side and it was Asteria's turn.

More confident and calmer than me, she walked along the narrow passage and came to my side while our feathered friend was following her every step. We were moving along the tunnel and was having all my senses alert.

We walked a lot among the stalactites and stalagmites having a spectacular view, but for the present I couldn't enjoy that so I went passed them without actually noticing them like I would do other times. However, some were so beautiful that you couldn't resist looking at them for a second time.

It was dark, which made it difficult for us to walk. We had to stop and wait on the other side or move forward very cautiously. I preferred the first option because I didn't know what to anticipate in the dark.

So, I told Asteria to stop at a place where was a kind of chamber formed and I sat on the ground at a corner. I couldn't bear the exhaustion I felt together with the humidity and heat which made it difficult for us to breathe. Our feathered friend had found a good place on Asteria's shoulder and soon our eyes closed.

I don't know how long I had been sleeping when I suddenly felt a cold current and sensed another presence in the place except for Asteria and me. I opened my eyes and I saw two indefinable shadows standing up. I looked more closely at them as much as that was possible.

"Son", I heard and recognized my father's voice.

"Father", I shouted. "You? Here?"

"Yes, we have come with your mother from the world of shadows, to see you", he said.

"Mother", I said with great longing.

"Son", I heard her saying. "I want to hold you tight so much, but I can't."

"Come closer mum", I screamed and tears rolled on my cheeks.

"It's better if you only hear us without looking at us because you will be disappointed by the sight", she said.

"I don't care. I just want to touch you", I replied.

"Don't ask something that is impossible, beyond reality in the world of spirits. It's enough that you can hear us," was the harsh response.

My tears were rolling non-stop, my sobbing was rocking my chest as I was bringing back to my memory happy moments of my life.

"Son", I heard my father saying, "you shouldn't put your life in danger anymore."

"But father, I have a mission to carry out", I replied.

"Your safety is more important. This mission is very dangerous and danger is lurking everywhere. We are worried about you", he said.

"So, father, are you telling me to stay in the world of spirits?" I asked.

"I'm not saying that",he said. "What I'm telling you is not to end up in Chaos if you don't make it."

"Mother, what do you think?" I asked her in agony as the tension that overwhelmed me, because of this unexpected meeting , had exhausted me emotionally.

"I agree with your father, son", she replied. "If you go to Chaos in the end, then it is better to stay here so that we will also have the chance to see you."

"So, do you mean I should refuse the real world to which I really wanted to return? Do you know that this is my last thought at night and my first when I wake up and that I have so many dreams for my life? It's not right to give up without trying. If I fail, at least I will be able to say that I have done the best I could, I fought but lost and I will be with clear conscience", I said.

"Your mother, that gave you life and raised you, is giving you some advice. Do you think she wants what is bad for you?" My mother replied.

"But, mother, I don't want to give up without fighting. I want to fight", I said.

"And what if this battle is already lost", said my father and stopped.

"Forgive me, but hypotheses and speculations are not enough for me. I want to live. Live!" I shouted loudly and with determination waking up Asteria who was next to me. She grabbed my arm and I couldn't understand why she did that.

"Then, we can't help you", said my father.

"Mother", I said, "haven't you got anything to say?"

"Since you have decided to abandon us and put your life at risk, what can I say?" She said.

"Mother, this is not true", I said while Asteria was still pulling my hand without understanding why.

"You are sending us away, with your behavior", said my mother. "It's as if you are saying that you don't want to see us."

"Don't give me dilemmas, I have decided to give it a try, because I want to live in the real world more rather than in the world of spirits", I replied. "I don't want to let all my effort and all that I have achieved so far go to waste."

"You are cruel and thoughtless of us", said my father. "You have always done things your way."

"Father, don't take things the wrong way. I will keep on fighting till the end. I'm sorry but for the first time I won't listen to you", I said. "I will trace my own road. I have my dreams and I want to delete them. It breaks my heart that I am raising my voice against your will but my logic imposes me to do so. I will fight till the end."

On my last words the figures of my parents began to change color and became purple while their faces were lit up and I could see the appalling figures of the demons.

"You are not my parents", I shouted after my discovery with feelings of fear and exasperation.

"You are walking towards chaos and you don't want to admit it", said one of them.

"For as long as you still have time, change your mind and quit", said the other "and Nohra will reward you."

"Never", I shouted. "I'd rather go to chaos rather than give it up crying like a coward."

"So, you will accept the consequences", said the first and disappeared with a flash and then the second left in the same way.

Only then did I realize the reason why Asteria was pulling my arm. She could see them in their real figures but I couldn't. I asked her and she confirmed. My head was about to break. My veins would be thrown out because of the tension and I could hear something buzzing as if a swarm of bees lived in my head.

I leaned, closed my eyes and let the tears roll. I really wanted to cry because the nostalgia and the memories from the familiar voices of my parents had brought back to my mind emotional and dear moments. The tears relieved me of my burden and I calmed down. Asteria, apparently, didn't understand what was happening to me neither was I in the mood to explain. I stayed in that position until my eyes closed.

That test didn't have an end. After so many obstacles and hardship I didn't know if I was close to my atonement or I had a long way ahead of me. I knew that Nohra and his demons wouldn't quit that easily and they would try to obstruct me in every way they could.

We moved forward to an underground tunnel and the humidity had become our second skin. Suddenly there was a roar like the one we heard in the beginning when the skeletons were getting out of the ground waking up from their eternal sleep. The ground was shaking more and more and something was about to come out. The temperature was dangerously high and the clothes were stuck on our body. However, what was coming from the depths was heard from behind not in front of us.

I decided that we should walk faster so as to avoid coming across it. We ran wherever that was possible and walked a bit faster wherever it was difficult. The underground tunnel was becoming narrower and I was afraid that if it ended up in a dead end we wouldn't have another way to escape and we would be like mice in a trap.

We reached the end of the tunnel which was closed by a rock but still had a small opening below near the ground. I ran in agony to see if it would be possible for us to pass successfully and fortunately it could fit one person. We crawled and passed one at a time while the underground roar was heard below us.

We got to a big chamber. We took a breath and carried on. As we were proceeding I was thinking of various things. How did the people of Okria come and put the metal here? Were we in the right way? When would we meet the chamber of the water?

Then I thought about my things, I was angry with God again who wasn't fair at all with making me go through an adventure like this against my will. Unfortunately, no matter what I thought of and what conclusion I came to, it wouldn't answer my queries about my situation.

We had passed the middle of the chamber when the vibration suddenly became deafening. The earth was shaking and we ran faster because the ground was lifting. We ran to the opposite direction when a fiery hell got out of the ground opening the crater.

Fire was jumping and passing everything; making the atmosphere feel like oven because of the high temperature. There was a smell of sulfur everywhere and fire was coming out non-stop.

We went to other side of the chamber which was becoming narrower ending up in a tunnel again and got back to see what would happen. The flames stopped coming out of the crater and started running separately like clouds, like big birds on the cove of the chamber. Like a big school of fiery fish, they were roaming and suddenly stopped and began assembling before our astonished eyes. Something huge and appalling was shaping. They were mingling and turning until they produced the desired result.

A huge fiery creature was completed and we could hear roars on its birth. I had never imagined a similar thing, not even in my dreams. We squeezed behind a rock and watched speechless at what was happening. There were three flames left moving around the huge monster and didn't go closer. It was screaming making the chamber shake.

It had a human body as far as I could tell because it was standing on two feet and it gave the impression it was fighting with an invisible enemy. It was attacking left and right without reason, throwing itself onto the walls of the cave then turning around itself as if something was bothering it. Suddenly, three flames jumped onto it. Two of them on its eyes and the third on its chest. Its screaming echoed and the invisible battle stopped for a moment. It stood on its feet and looked at the place we were sitting and began roaring; coming towards us. We used all the power and stamina we had in order to escape.

But we didn't know where to go. The unknown was in front of us and behind us that fiery hell chasing us. We were running non-stop out of breath with the fright written in our eyes and the fire coming nearer. It didn't have to touch us. We would be burning soon because of the high temperature. The only thing that would save us would be to find the chamber of water.

We got to a narrow passage and moved on. Behind us the fiery creature had no difficulty in passing as well. It was obvious that it wouldn't take long. We didn't have so much power anymore and the fiery monster was dangerously close to us. Finally the narrow passage opened and a big chamber appeared. To my disappointment it wasn't the chamber of water.

I had a look around but I could see no exit. So that was the end. That was the furthest we could go. I bore the obstacles and challenges. It was simply the end.

I looked around in despair to see something that would give me hope that I would be saved, but in vain. Asteria would suffer too because of me. That poor girl had run and squeezed in a curve of a rock and waited for the end to come. I went there too, while our feathered friend never left Asteria's shoulder even though it could fly and save itself.

The fiery monster had got into from the narrow part of the cave and stood in the middle examining the area. As soon as it tracked us down, it made a few more steps towards us and stopped again. It screamed and a hot breath of Liva (a southwesterly Mediterranian wind) got out of its mouth. It moved a few more steps towards us and its temperature was burning us.

We stuck onto the walls of the cave with our backs against the wall waiting for the fatal to happen. Asteria was behind me and I was at the front unable; at the mercy of the fire. The monster made another step and smelled my hair burning. I closed my eyes so that I wouldn't see and suddenly I lost my balance and fell causing a loud noise with my falling.

Asteria fell down with me when the wall of that curve we were leaning moved because, as we discovered, it was the entrance which had been closed by someone from inside with a sheet of rock. We gained an extension of life and the fiery monster stood indecisive.

We stood up and I thought of removing the sheet of rock, placing it again in order to block the entrance again but it was only a thought. It was so heavy that

I would need more than five men to move it. I looked around to see where we were and realized that we were at the chamber of water at last!

There was indeed a pond in the cave we had got into, and in its middle there was a column and on its top there was a stone statue of a griffin. So we were at the end but the final result was still unknown. Finally on the other bank of the lake there was an altar and nothing else. I had to decide what we would do quickly.

"Into the water", I screamed at Asteria, seeing no other solution as the fiery monster was getting in.

We fell into water while our feathered friend was flying above us. The monster remained indecisive but when it decided to come near us I told Asteria to dive our heads into the water holding our breath. The monster, instead of touching us, touched the water and we saw it giving out smoke. It tried again with the same result. I noticed that every time it touched the water, it became smaller. So after many attempts, it had lost one third of its size and looked weak.

After a few more unsuccessful attempts, we saw it moving to the centre and blowing up like a firework producing a big bang filling the chamber with smoke. The fiery nightmare had disappeared. We got out of the water and then a voice out of nowhere was heard.

"Do you know how long I had been waiting for this moment?" The voice said.

I turned towards the direction where the voice was heard from and to my amazement I saw the griffin which was on top of the column having turned to our direction. It was a demon after all which pretending to be a statue, I thought. It immediately flew and landed in the entrance blocking our exit. It changed its appearance and I recognized Nohra.

"I had warned you", he said "but you thought you were strong enough to fight with me. I admit that I have admired your courage and boldness so far but there is a limit in everything. There is an end in everything. Because I wasn't sure that the Pyrikaphsto, the spirit of the volcanoes that I had sent, would carry out its mission, I decided to wait for you here, because I wanted to have the pleasure of being present at the final battle. Have a nice trip in Chaos", it said, going to the entrance towards the previous chamber. It stood there, raised his hands lifting them slowly.

The big sheet of rock that had fallen, was lifted slowly and blocked the entrance, while his laughter was heard as the earth started shaking.

"Earthquake", I said.

It was indeed a strong earthquake that lasted a long time. Huge rocks were falling from the ceiling and we were running to save ourselves. Rocks fell onto the entrance, sealing it. The water of the pond disappeared suddenly into the depths of the earth and we gathered at a corner as we were in real danger. The earthquake continued and the column that was shaking leaned, fell down and smashed into pieces.

I felt pain below my knee and saw my leg bleeding. A piece of the column that had broken hit me there. It wasn't a big wound but it really hurt. The capital on the top of the statue broke in two pieces as it fell and one part of it rolled towards our side. In it we saw the connection, that is the melted metal which had in its centre so that it could be joined with the other pieces of the column. Then I noticed something that was shining.

"The gold metal", I said, and showed it to Asteria in no mood at all. 'The metal inside the metal' as the oracle said. For that thing I had gone through so much to find it and now that I did, it was useless. What would I do with it since there was no way we could escape? We would die here without having anyone to help us.

The vibrations from the earthquake had ceased and the air was full of dust. I didn't have the courage to think nor to speak. So, out of curiosity, I pulled out the gold metal, held it in my hands for a while, and then threw it away. I heard Asteria crying and praying on her knees. I felt so sorry for her that I went near her and hugged her.

"I'm asking you to forgive me", I said, "for bringing you in this situation, and if it were up to me, I would never allow this to happen."

The sobbing was shaking her body and I couldn't bear it because I felt so guilty and because I had no dreams anymore. There was no hope. Our feathered friend was flying above us, probably sensing how tragic the situation was. We were buried alive in the depths of the earth condemned to die slowly.

I stood up and held Asteria's hand. She was the one who hadn't broken down even once. She hadn't shed a tear. She hadn't complained about anything even though she had suffered so much. And now she couldn't stop crying.

Suddenly, she left my side and ran into the altar to pray again. Poor girl. She was praying to God for help in vain. God's power couldn't reach this place.

Then Asteria stood up and something weird happened. She held the square sheet of stone which was in the altar and tried to turn it. I don't know if it was an illusion or reality because I was so desperate, but it seemed to me that it moved.

"Come", she made a gesture with her hand.

I went nearer and realized that it had really moved. What did she have in mind? What was she trying to do? She made gesture to me again to go and try to turn it. I held it from its corners and with all my power I felt it turning as if it were unscrewing. I turned it twice and it was gone completely. I lifted it and it was miracle! There was a drop with steps that were going downwards.

I hugged Asteria again and her sobbing became more intense. I couldn't explain her reaction. Since she knew that secret with the altar, it meant that it led to a salvation exit. So why was she crying?

She got in first but I ran to get the gold metal that I had thrown before following her. She made a gesture telling me to put the sheet back to its place. Indeed, those who had built that secret entrance, had thought that it should have four bumps from inside so that someone can close it from inside.

On every step we were going down, Asteria's crying became more intense. The steps finished and we walked through a small corridor and then we found steps again that were going up this time. The wound on my leg had stopped bleeding but it was still hurting me. But that was of little importance to me.

We began descending and Asteria didn't stop crying. The steps finished but there was no exit. Then Asteria asked me, with a gesture, to push the ceiling above my head. When I did it a square sheet of stone appeared. I lifted it carefully and something that really impressed me appeared.

There was a chamber that looked like a dome above us, in which I noticed at a glance the statue of Agitoras Apollo, that we had seen at Agitoria, hanging. So, if I understood correctly, we were under the Temple of Agitoras Apollo or somewhere near there.

We got onto the chamber and I was ecstatic with what I saw. The chamber had a big round table with seven seats in its center. The center of the table, which had a diameter of about four or five meters, was empty and at a lower level there was an unbelievable object. A rock that I would call 'airstone' because it was round from its nature in dark brown color; as if it had fallen from the sky.

It wasn't carved because I could see a few imperfections and cracks. The most impressive thing of all though,was that there was a golden river flowing inside it like a wide strip about two inches, which was wider at some points and narrower at others, shining. At the center of the ceiling there was an opening from where the sun was going in shining on the gold metal which was reflecting light.

I was magnetized by the spectacle but Asteria's crying brought me back to my senses, watching her running towards the statue of God which was on the wall. Our feathered friend had left Asteria's shoulder and started flying in circles as if it were dancing on the dome. Then it approached Asteria, made a few circles flying around it and then to me, and finally it flew through the ceiling and disappeared. Asteria had fallen on the floor in front of the statue crying with sobs. I went near her, lifted her softly and held her tenderly.

"Why", I asked her. "Why are you crying?"

She turned her head and looked at me with a sad look with those big blue eyes of hers and then she left and went to a small door that was near. She opened it and I followed her. We climbed up a few steps and I had to lift another sheet of stone from the ceiling.

As soon as I did that, we were at a familiar place which I had visited with Head Priestess Psamanthi. In the room with the two carved monoliths from the first worship of the sun in Symi, so, we were in the Temple of Agitoras Apollo in which Asteria was a Priestess.

That moment, before I finished putting the sheet back to its place, a Priestess appeared and after making a shout, she disappeared running. It seems that she went to announce the fact that we were alive from the depths of the Underworld. I couldn't believe it.

I had completed the seventh test and I had every reason to be happy. I would go back to my normal life, to the things I loved, to what I had fought for until now thanks to Asteria. But her attitude didn't let me feel happy for the outcome of my efforts. As we were about to get out of the room with the monoliths, two priests got in a hurry, grabbed Asteria and dragged her out by force before my astonished eyes.

"But, what are you doing", I screamed as they were leaving.

"It's none of your business", replied one of them.

Asteria turned and gave a last look full of complaint that killed me psychologically. I couldn't understand what they were thinking. What had the girl done and took her like that as if she were a criminal? I got out and saw Aetion.

"They are waiting for you in the Temple to give them the metal", he said.

"Aren't we going to the Temple of Miragetis Apollo to Hyperinor?" I asked.

"No, Mystic Hyperinor is here waiting for you", he answered.

I got into the Temple hesitantly and saw Mystic Ioxos walking about very nervous and Mystic Hyperinor was sitting on a chair looking very distant and dark. I bowed and offered him the pot with the metal inside. He took it and showed me the door without saying anything.

I didn't expect such behavior towards me. What had we done? Very troubled for the ambiance there, I got out of the Temple and left with Aetion going to Okria. I had so many questions which I asked him to answer me but he was numb.

"But, what happened?" I asked.

"Nothing that has to do with you", he said.

"I hope that nothing has changed and I will return to the real world", I replied.

"I have no convincing answers on that question either", he said.

I was scared to death about my future and I was returning to Okria with my head boiling and the worst psychology. I was expecting the moment that I would complete all the tests to be different and now I feel as I am in prison waiting for the judges' verdict.

CHAPTER 27

We returned to Okria and I was left alone, with the true meaning of the word. There was not enough space in the room for my loneliness nor my sorrow. My future was uncertain and I was empty inside. I missed so many things. Maybe because I needed to look at them, touch them, feel that I was in the real world.

On the other hand, I couldn't understand the attitude of the others towards Asteria and somewhere deep inside, I felt that this bad behavior against her was partly my fault. I was sure that it had something to do with me. But in what way?

I was trying to understand where I was wrong or what she had done wrong but I couldn't get any convincing answers. I had the urge to go out. To find Hyperinor and talk to him and ask for explanations. I couldn't bear this anticipation and silence. It was killing me. But I didn't dare do it.

I was dug into the room like a mole, with my self-destructive thoughts and agony for company. I was in there for so many hours. When there was a knock on the door, these knocks had the same effect that the pebbles have in a small calm lake.

All my feelings burst at once, to guess and explain the reason of that visit. Was it good or bad? What was I about to hear? I opened the door hesitantly but in anticipation and saw Aetion.

"Come", he said. "Let's go."

"Where?" I asked.

"To the chamber of the people where you had been the first time you came to Okria", said Aetion.

I followed him hesitantly and we passed, like the first time, through various doors, caves and corridors until we arrived at a big door. Aetion opened it and we got in. Everyone was at their positions. He left me at the same point he had done the first time and took his position on the heroes' seats.

Hyperinor was very thoughtful and everyone looked worried. I could see that in their silent chats, their gestures and the seriousness on their faces. My agony was on its peak as I was waiting for what I had to hear. What had they finally decided for me? Would they let me go or would I stay in Okria forever as I could assume from the previous signs? Hyperinor stood up and everyone was silent.

Hyperinor began saying:

"I want to talk to you about some events that have taken place and announce you my decisions and a few other things. Always having the good of Okria as our first priority we are gathered here today, to make decisions on crucial issues. With the help of Apollo, we will carry on our life in the place we love and have never abandoned.

You all know that we have lost one of our people when he went to reality on a mission holding our symbol which someone else found and was found here unexpectedly. Our decision for him was to stay in Okria, unless he wanted to return to the real world - which he did - so he had to go through seven tests. Find the seven metals that compose the symbol of Okria so that he would be able to return to his world. He is here with us now, since he has completed his mission and passed all the tests."

A whisper of admiration was heard by the crowd and everyone looked at me thoroughly. I remember back then, the first time they laughed when I said that I wanted to try and go through the tests.

"You have before you, the man who will be called a 'hero' from now on because he was able to resist and overcome the obstacles of Nohra's demons showing remarkable courage and bravery", he said.

"The name that he will have here in Okria and which he will carry with him from now on is the name of the son of the sun 'Marathos'. We want him here in Okria because he has proved that he is a fighter and has will and persistence in everything he attempted. But if he doesn't want to stay, the procedures for his returning to his world will now begin", said Hyperinor.

"Marathos", he said addressing to me, "what is your decision? Are you staying with us or go to your world?"

"I want to return to my world", I said, as fast as I could, with no second thoughts or hesitation.

"Then, tomorrow the procedures for what you long for and what you have fought for, shall begin", he replied.

Hearing that, a wave of joy overwhelmed me and blew my mind. I would return to my world! I wanted to run and hug all of them, even the ones I didn't know, to greet them and tell them that I was returning!!! I was happy, filled with joy and couldn't wait to say goodbye to the world of Okria.

So it was unfair of me to doubt their trustworthiness and the prevalence of justice. All the heartbeats, the doubts and anticipation weren't justified. I was returning!!! Aetion asked me to go out. I bowed in front of the Mystics, thanked them and got out with Aetion.

"If you want", he said, "you can wait for the meeting to end and then we can go but you can return to your room on your own. You know the way now so you don't need me."

"I want to say goodbye to some of them before I leave", I said.

"We have the time", he answered and left.

I decided to return on my own and stay in the room, to share the joy only with myself and recollect the moments I had lived. I arrived in Okria with no surprises and got into the room. I was thinking of who I would say to goodbye to on my leaving. First of all Asteria whom I didn't see in the chamber, Aetion, Mystic Hyperinor and Head Priestess Psamanthi.

The truth is that Asteria and I went through a lot. She experienced with me all the difficult and pleasant moments during the trials and went through many bad things because of me. Without complaining. Without grumbling. Without letting signs of exhaustion and disappointment show on her face. She was always there for me following the instructions she had been given. A special, rare character. I would like a girl like her as a wife in the real world.

I remember how bad I felt when I discovered that she couldn't talk. That disability of hers made me like her even more. I don't know if I searched deep inside me, if I would find that there was something more than just 'likeness'. But something like that could never blossom in two different worlds. Either I should stay in Okria or she should come to the real world, which was not just difficult, it was impossible.

I brought back to my memory moments of my tests on which the two of us had come closer and, I have to say, there was a certain feeling of embarrassment not only from my side but also for hers too.

On the third test with the electric fish of Nanou, where one had to drag the other ashore after the heating and the numbness from the fish so that we wouldn't drown. Our contact really overwhelmed me but I tried to hide it because it was another test for me that I had to go through.

On the fifth test, at the entrance of the precipice, where the demons had hung her from her hair on the tree I had to take her in my arms, untie her hair and place her safely on the ground. Again I had the same feeling and embarrassment.

On the last test, after the earthquake, when we were buried alive in the depths of the earth, where she started crying and praying, I hugged her to comfort her and give her courage. The same feeling again.

But why did I bring these to my memory? Because simply, I don't have the agony and the doubts for my future. Because now I know the decision for my return and free from all the negative thoughts, I can now recollect those moments.

There was also that crazy idea that I had seen her somewhere before. Is it possible with this difference of two thousand years between us and I believed that I had seen that girl in my world? There were many times that I was secretly observing her, trying to guess where I had seen her. I never managed to remember.

With all this joy for the happy news, I forgot to ask Aetion about Asteria. The last scene I have from her in my eyes and it is carved in my memory, is when the Priests took her and she turned to look at me. That look of hers penetrated me like a knife. It was as if she was saying goodbye to me forever, and she was begging me and expressing complaint.

But why did they treat her like that? I will definitely ask tomorrow to find out more details. Besides, I want to see her before I leave. If it is necessary I will go myself to the Temple of Agitoras Apollo.

CHAPTER 28

It was the first time I had slept so peacefully. Maybe because I didn't have the agony and the stress of the test like before, neither the worrying about my future. I woke up in a happy mood waiting for Aetion who came soon.

"Get ready Marathos", he said, using the name Hyperinor had given me.

"I am ready", I replied, full of joy.

"I will come by in a while and we will leave", said Aetion.

As he was leaving, I remembered of Asteria and I called him.

"I forgot to ask how Asteria is doing", I said. "I want to say goodbye to her."

"It's a bit difficult", he said, hesitating to finish his sentence.

"Why is it hard?" I asked.

"You don't really need to know", he said, making me think of the worst.

"Speak clearly", I said. "Is there something wrong? Why did the three priestesses take her when we got out of the Temple of Agitoras Apollo?"

"Do you really want to know the truth?" he asked.

"Of course I do", I said.

"It will make you sad", he replied.

"Now I want it even more", I said, however hard it would be.

"She is on trial at the moment in the chamber of the people with the charge of perjury", he told me.

"Why?" I asked.

"Because she revealed the secret passage to you in order to reach the statue of the God. Something which she had taken an oath before the God and the Mystics that she wouldn't do for as long as she lived", Aetion replied.

"But if she hadn't done it, we would have died in the depths of the earth", I said.

"It would be preferable rather than breaking her oath to God", responded Aetion.

"And what will they do to her?" I asked.

Aetion simply replied, "the punishment will be to die at the stake."

I wasn't prepared to hear something like that so I went back terrified. I held on the door and my heart was beating like a drum and my stomach hurt as if it had been punched. It was impossible for me to accept this. At least up to the point that was up to me, I would do anything to cancel this conviction.

"Let's go to the chamber", I said.

"You can't change the decisions", he said. "It's pointless."

"No, I want to go and explain to Hyperinor and the Mystics", I said.

Aetion started unwillingly while I was running even faster to make it before the decision and on my mind I thought of the way I would defend her. When we got there, the people were leaving, which was a sign that the decision had been made and I didn't manage to save Asteria. My feet were shaking but I made an effort to go in, pushing the people and screaming, "wait, wait…"

Some of them looked at me strangely, others were smiling. The Mystics were about to go down and Asteria was leaving the room escorted by two guards.

"Wait", I shouted.

They all turned to look at me.

"Wait", I screamed again. "You can't make this decision."

"Why?" Asked Hyperinor.

"Because you don't know exactly how the things happened to be able to make the right decision", I replied.

"The fact that she didn't keep her oath to God is enough", said Hyperinor. The rest aren't necessary.

"But would it have been preferable if we had died in the depths of the earth?" I asked.

"It would be more preferable than breaking her oath", he replied.

"I think you are being unfair", I said. "I was mistaken to believe that you weren't. In the end Nohra may not be completely wrong."

"How dare you say something like that?" Said one of the Mystics.

"I dare to do so, because I hate injustice and being absolute. All this story happened because of me and Asteria is being accused because of me. You have to be lenient", I said.

"The rules are rules and the decisions don't change. No one has reversed that so far", he replied.

"I will argue for the event so that the judgment will be fair", I replied.

"You are not on trial for something that you haven't done", he reminded me.

"Yes but Asteria is in this situation because of me. So I am partly guilty too", I said.

"You haven't taken an oath", said the Mystic.

"But I would do the same if the life of both of us was in danger. She didn't do it to save herself only", I replied.

There was silence and Hyperinor sat and looked at the person on his right and then on his left and they whispered something. My agony for Asteria's luck was immense. After consultation among the groups of seven, nine and twelve heroes, Hyperinor said, "the decision can change only when the one who had got to know illegally the sanctuary of the God, never leaves Okria."

That decision was a slap in my face. It was very cruel. I had to renounce the real world throwing all my fighting, my trying and trials into waste. I was dreaming of the day, the hour, the moment of my return for so many days and nights, and now I would have to forget about my desire which had given me the courage to resist and fight the demons of Nohra?

I was in a big dilemma. Either I would have to let Asteria go to Chaos and I would return to my world that I wanted so much. Or I would stay in Okria to save her. It wasn't a decision I could make right away. It wasn't a simple answer. It required much thought and concentration. It was a matter of life and death. But I had to decide at that moment.

"So, why do you care if Asteria goes to chaos", a low voice inside me was heard saying, your survival comes first.

"That's a shame", answered another voice loudly. "You were the one that was fighting for justice, freedom and equality for everyone, and now you will allow a weak girl to be sentenced to death because of something she has done to save your life?"

"Or the values you believe in are only for the stories you make up for the others?"

But I have gone through so much to come to this day and return to my world. I agreed with the first voice.

"And will you bear to think that you were the reason for someone's death?" said the second voice.

No one will ever have to know, I thought.

"But I will know and will remind you frequently because I am your conscience. You will be the murderer of Asteria unless you help her", said the second voice.

Oh God! What will I do? My feelings were mixed. I was divided in two. What should I decide?

"Murderer" I heard the one voice screaming at me.

"Live the real life, that you have gone through so much in order to conquer it", said the other voice.

"Murderer", my conscience continued. "You have nice words only for the others. When it comes to you to make decision you change like the chameleon."

Should I quit life for ever?

"Send the girl to death, murderer", said the first voice.

"Stop", I screamed.

"What did you say?" Asked a Mystic.

"When I stay here, what will happen to Asteria?" I asked.

"She will remain where she used to be", said Hyperinor.

I looked inside me to see what the logic and my heart were telling me to do, but it was all fifty-fifty. As usual, on the first thought the feeling was faster covering the logic. On the second though, the logic imposed its opinion.

Everyone was looking at me and everyone was waiting for my answer. I looked at Asteria hesitantly. She was bowed and melancholic, anticipating either her death or her salvation and I was the one that would decide that. The help she had offered me secretly despite her oath, came to my mind, when she showed me how to escape from the altar when I had no hope to be saved.

I shouldn't think about it too much. She had given me life at least twice, and I couldn't decide what to do. But all I longed for and fought for would be erased with one word? I was about to mouth the word and at the last minute I regretted it. That moment Asteria turned and our eyes met.

"I will stay", I shouted.

All you could hear was an 'AAAAAA!!!!!'' in the room and everyone stood up. The Mystics, the heroes, the twelve and the crowd, were clapping but my heart was as black as coal. But I owed it to Asteria after all she had done for me.

The clapping went on, incessant and there were cheers. It was paradoxical, tragic and oxymoronic. These clapping and cheering were an award for my death. When the applause stopped, the Mystics were silent as if they were thinking as I could see from their face. As if they were meditating and then Hyperinor spoke.

"Marathos", he said, "has proved again that the physical power is not as important as the will of the mind and the values that discriminate the human from the other creatures. And because here in Okria we think values are more important, according to

God Apollo, we acknowledge the strength of his soul to sacrifice himself in order to save Priestess Asteria, even though he fought going through all the tests in order to return where he wanted, we will free him and allow him to return to his world on one condition. If he promises and swears to Apollo that he will never reveal the secret for which Asteria was accused."

The emotional changes were so intense that if they could be shown in color, I would change color every second. It was as if I was having a shower with cold water and then with hot. From nadir to zenith and backwards. I couldn't believe what I was hearing. What Hyperinor said, was music to my ears. I turned to Asteria but she had disappeared.

"So? What is your decision?" Hyperinor said.

"I promise I will never reveal that secret and I will swear before God and the people", I said.

"When the sun on its higher point, be at the Temple of Parnopios Apollo in Marathounda, which is dedicated to Lycious Apollo together with another one and they are ruins now. There, you will take an oath to God and leave for your world. The assembling is over", he said.

Then Aetion got down and as the people were leaving the room, he said to me, "whatever you have achieved, you have achieved it with your abilities. I admired you for your brave decision but I am sorry that Okria will lose such a great man."

"Thank you for your kind words, even though I had doubts for you during that incident with Nohra", I replied.

"Never mind. I would have done the same", he said.

There was silence for a while and I was looking at the people who were leaving, trying to see Asteria. I finally asked Aetion.

"I think that after the announcement that you could return to your world, she returned on her duties", said Aetion.

"I want to see her and say goodbye to her." I told him.

"She will probably be going to the Temple of Agitoras. But, you know, now that her mission to accompany you on your tests is over, it is hard for you to meet each other because the Priestesses aren't allowed to have contacts outside their temples and beyond their duties", said Aetion.

"I understand that but I just want to say goodbye to her", I replied.

"I will transfer your wish to Hyperinor", said Aetion.

"OK, but I don't have much time at my disposal. Besides, we have to go to Marathounda from Okria for the ceremony of my going back to reality." I reminded him.

"We will bear that in mind", he said and we separated.

I returned to my room with a mixture of feelings of joy, worrying, agony, anticipation, impatience, and a bit of a gap and emptiness at a part of my mind. I couldn't organize all I had inside me. I looked at the bed, the table and the seats for the last time. The blue sphere which was floating above my bed after the end of my seventh test had disappeared when I returned.

How many heartbeats, agonies, anticipations I had gone through in that room made of stone and how many times I had gone through the pages of the book of my life in order to hold on to something and avoid being driven mad because of this crazy situation I was in.

"I am leaving", I said loudly as if I wanted myself to confirm this, to hear it and believe that this paranoia was over.

I don't know, but somewhere in the bottom of my heart I was leaving a part of me here. It was the moments I had shared with Asteria, the dangers, the happy and sad moments, the disappointments and the successes of the tests.

The touring in my mind ended by Aetion who spoke to me. "We are leaving" he said, and gave me my clothes. I changed, I looked around the room for the last time and closed the door.

The sun was high and everything was golden. We set off for Marathounda, for the Temple of Parnopios Apollo and as we were passing through a narrow passage on the mountain top we saw Marathounda bay, peaceful and tranquil. I was going down silent, full of thoughts about many things.

I brought Asteria back to my mind and the moments she was crying at the underground cave after the earthquake and I connected it with her trial. Then, I understood why she was crying and praying.

It wasn't because she was weak or she was asking for help as I thought then. Her tears were her way to ask for forgiveness because she was breaking an oath she had taken that she wouldn't reveal the inaccessible with the statue of the God. That's why her crying went on even after we had gone out of the cave, even though I couldn't understand it then. She must have fought inside her a great deal to do such a thing against what the God ordered. It required a big decision and will but mainly a big heart.

We arrived at the Temple which was a pile of ruins but a square monolith was standing at the centre like an altar on which I could discern the symbol of Okria. All the Mystics were there discussing.

"I don't see Asteria", I said to Aetion in a low voice.

He didn't reply and went to Hyperinor and whispered something to him. He nodded his head while the other Mystics were taking their position forming a circle around the monolith with the symbol. They probably didn't want me to see Asteria, I thought to myself. That's unfair. But there was no way I could change it. Aetion left and I was alone with the Mystics.

Hyperinor came close to me and looking at me in the eye he said:

> "You have beaten all the fears that can be in the human mind since the man appeared on Earth for the first time. The unknown in life, the death, the luck, elements and phenomenon of nature. Unknown worlds of the visible and invisible, magic powers, creatures of the fantasy and powers of darkness. Heroes are like that. To make the impossible possible in the battle against the evil that surrounds us and attacks us every day.
>
> I'm glad you came into our world because I know that you had it on your mind since you were a young boy without knowing if it

really existed. That's why the great honor of returning to Okria if you ever want it, will be given only to you by reciting the following - 'Holding the trace of the symbol on the stone at the four points of the horizon, on the day when there is no shade and by saying backwards (from the end to the beginning) the solar myth of birth.'

"I don't know if I will ever want to return here again after all that I had been through", I said.

"Maybe, someday, you will want it", he replied.

"Neither do I know the solar myth", I said.

He said, "there will be signs that will reveal it to you."

There was silence and Hyperinor said, "in order to return to your world, you will follow this procedure: you will stand beside the altar, showing the big square monolith to me, with your hands touching the symbol of Okria which is carved on it at the four parts of the horizon."

I rallied all the courage I had and I said, "I had the wish to say goodbye to Asteria but that was impossible in the end."

"I notified her", said Hyperinor.

I knew there was nothing more I could say, so I remained silent having a complaint for this story. I looked at the path from which we had descended from Okria and I saw something moving high up. Could it be Asteria? Who knew? But even if it was her, she wouldn't make it because Hyperinor made a gesture to me to put my hands on the carved symbol.

The Mystics were at their positions and my heart was beating fast because of the procedure and also for the fact that Asteria wouldn't make it in the end. Suddenly it got darker and darker and the stars rose in the sky. The Mystics were holding the sacred pots with the metals in their hands reaching out, when I heard a voice calling my name.

"Marathos, Marathos!"

I turned to the direction where the voice was coming from and I saw Asteria running and approaching while the Mystics had already started the procedure and a whisper of words I couldn't understand like a prayer was heard.

"Asteria", I shouted.

"It's me, Marathos", I heard her answering, surprised without believing my ears.

"Can you talk?" I asked her; impressed and happy with this discovery.

"I have always talked, but I had taken an oath not to say a word for as long as I would be with you. I have come to thank you for everything you have done for me", she revealed.

I was about to say something but a breeze blew outside the circle of the Mystics and the whispers became voices and you thought they were saying verses of an epic. It must be the solar myth, I thought to myself.

In the meantime there were electric evacuations from the pots they were holding small in the beginning and bigger later on and they were coming towards me. The wind outside the Mystics' circle had become a whirlwind blowing on their tunics and hair in a scenery that made me a bit scared.

I turned to Asteria again, as the electric evacuations were joining at the center of the monolith on the carved symbol of Okria and I felt exactly as I felt when I had found the symbol; that I was going into fog losing my conscience.

"Marathos", I heard Asteria, but didn't have the power to reply.

I tried to open my eyes and heard a voice calling my name again but louder this time.

"Marathos, Marathos."

I finally opened my eyes and saw Asteria standing beside me, looking at me and smiling with those big eyes of hers.

"It's about time you woke up", I heard her saying.

"Where am I?" I said half lost, having lost the track of time and space.

"In Marathounda", she replied.

She was dressed in different clothes now. She was wearing jeans and a white shirt and she was smiling. And the sun was behind her, it created bright shades that were playing around her body. Far away, the voices of the people who were lying on the beach of Marathounda, came to my ears as a music soundtrack for the image I had before my eyes.

"Asteria", I said. "How did you come to my world?"

"First of all, it is weird that you are calling me Asteria because I was given that name out of Symi and you shouldn't know that", she replied.

"OK, my turn to ask now. How did you call me Marathos, since my name is Michalis?" I asked.

"But that was the name I had given you when I was playing as a little girl and you were in my game", she said.

"What game?" I asked.

"Here on the rock of the beach of Marathounda. Don't you remember when we were kids and I was asking you to come and play with me but you wouldn't notice me?" She said.

"So it is you", I replied. And all that timeI was wondering who Asteria reminded me of.

"Yes, it's me", said Astradeni.

"Where have you been all this time?" I asked.

She explained, "I wasn't on Symi because we left after you. But when I returned, I fulfilled a promise I had given to the nine Temples of Archangelos Michail on the island and as I was passing by from here because I wanted to remember my childhood on the beach, someone told me that you were here. So I came and found you sleeping on this monolith."

There are nine Temples dedicated to Apollo and nine Temples dedicated to Archangelos Michail. That is a weird coincidence, I thought. I raised my head and looked at the upper part of the monolith. The symbol of Okria was indeed carved there. I had no doubts anymore. It all really happened. It wasn't my imagination.

But no one would believe that all this was true. Unless...... I looked at Asteria or Astradeni who was smiling, waiting for me to stand up reaching out her hand to me.

"We have got many things to say", I told her.

"Of course" she said. "Besides, you owe it to me since you were in my game but you kept ignoring me."

As she leaned on me reaching out her hand, I noticed that the necklace that could be seen from her shirt… It was the symbol of Okria!!!!

"Wait", I said. "Where did you find that necklace?"

"Well, you can't learn everything at once" she said. "We have to get to know each other again first and then I will tell you everything…"